BEOWULF

A Current English Version

Modernization by

David Kaufman

First Edition
ISBN: 978-0-6151-3758-2
Copyright © 2006, David Kaufman

For Alan Markman and Fr. Klaeber

In Payment of Old Debts

For Cari and Sean, with love . . . .

INTRODUCTION

* * * * * * * * * * * *

My introduction to BEOWULF was the typical one of most graduate students who get to a certain point in their academic careers -- if I wished to climb even just a little higher up the rocky path to literary wisdom, I would be forced to translate the thing. One quick look at the poem in the original and I could see with pristine clarity the formidable task I was in for. The words looked vaguely what I guessed Swedish might look like, not English at all, and while my feelings about that first shock have mellowed, I still suspect that I recognized the ontogenetic ancestor of only one word in, say, four or five dozen. But I dutifully began my hundred lines a day, excited, even eager about the long task ahead. Soon enough I was certain I would never reach that daily goal.

And it was not too much longer before I knew I would need some assistance.

I was going to need profound assistance, as a matter of fact.

Now, desperate graduate students use desperate measures, and so I found myself deep in the Hillman stacks, trying to look as scholarly and as sagacious as possible, trying to look as if I were in earnest pursuit of an essential piece of knowledge, but actually I was a student in search of a trot.

I decided upon two, the Thorpe and the Morgan.

Each translation is monumental; each was a great assist to me that very long semester. And because over the next few months I grew to love the poem and had a growing awareness of what that long gone and forever obscure West Saxon had in mind, I came to see clearly that while each translation is awesome, neither is BEOWULF.

The poem is not so lacking in transitional or connective tissue that it is nothing if it is not obscure, as Thorpe's rendition so often is, nor are the lines so elegant and so ennobled that the poem seems dainty and at times even effete, as Morgan's offering clearly suggests.

The Old English poem BEOWULF is a dignified, no nonsense statement about existence in a harsh and often bitter world, the hero himself the idealization of the attempt to survive in a place and time where bad things really did happen to a man who was unfortunate enough to be caught outside after dark. It is a story that would appeal to a people who wished at night to be under a roof and near the fire, and who grudgingly endured the cold but counted the passing of years by the harshest milestone they could think of -- the winter. The early audience knew well enough what the poet meant when he said, however figuratively, that Beowulf (and Hrothgar as well) ruled for fifty winters. And any modern reader who has read THE WANDERER knows that the BEOWULF poet's statement is a testament to courage and endurance as well as to political excellence.

In BEOWULF the cruel environment itself is so real that it is as much a character in the work as the heath is in Hardy, and it is equally central to the poem. The monsters, so important in BEOWULF, are the personification of that marvelous environment, and Beowulf's encounters with them account for almost all of the action and excitement of the poem.

There is a reason for that. For BEOWULF to survive orally, as it must have done in one form or another for years before a written version of any sort finally existed, it had to be popular at the level of folk literature, and it would not appeal to the early listener in any form but action. In those long winter nights with little to do but sit quietly and stare into the fire, few stories would be so attractive to him as one in which the hero not only endured his environment, but prevailed manfully against it.

And if in BEOWULF the poet meant to show that *lif is læne,* he succeeded admirably. Life is portrayed as harsh and unfair, the heroic effort in face of absurd odds the only means of significance, the only chance of vindication the fending off of whatever monsters came a man's way.

And so far as finding value in BEOWULF for the current reader, aside from the fact that it is a ripping good story, it has been suggested that each generation has its own set of monsters. For us, too, BEOWULF endorses the idea that the heroic approach to life is an honorable way to deal with matters over which we have no control.

While no justification for attempting to make such a work of art as BEOWULF more widely known is necessary, that display of heroic existentialism, if you will, was a large part of the motivation that got me through the task the first time around and much of what impelled me to attempt to bring the poem to a far more polished form now. I came to the end of the poem at least figuratively weeping, not only for Beowulf and the lesser heroes of that splendid poem, all of whom had been afforded the portion of *lof* they yearned for and deserved, but perhaps more for those long gone listeners of the story who had to endure an environment far more formidable than any I would ever know, most of whom likely got praise from no one for their efforts.

I'd have bought those guys a mead anytime.

David Kaufman,
Pittsburgh 2006

x

THE SUBJECT MATTER OF BEOWULF

* *

In all of the Western World there are few ideas more seminal to the advancement of civilization than the concept of the *comitatus*. Its tenets of loyalty, service, gift-giving for service, and mutual protection for king and retainer, constitute a splendidly thought out bulwark against the hostile environment, and it was the best chance of safety and even of survival for the members of the group. The concept can be inferred to be biological in nature, having origins at the very beginning of specialized life, when single-celled ciliates banded physically together and accepted specialized duties for the good of the new organism.

The idea of the *comitatus* is in fact so well developed in BEOWULF that early critics of the poem valued it more as a sociological treatise than as a piece of literature. Whatever the error of that initial conclusion, it is the truth that one would not need to go elsewhere in literature to find

the tenets of the *comitatus* so very handsomely set forth.   In
its essentials the *comitatus* requires mutual loyalty between
king and warrior, with protection, service, shelter, generosity
in feasting and gift giving -- all the essentials of civilization,
in fact, the communal goals.

Much of Hrothgar's anguish in the first part of the
poem stems from the fact that he cannot fulfill his warrants
to the *comitatus*; however loyal he is to his men, he can give
neither banquet nor treasure in Heorot because of the
continuing horror of Grendel. And they in turn have failed to
protect him. It is a society in turmoil, in danger of collapse.

Beowulf himself is the personification of the concept
of the hero warrior in the *comitatus*. The idea of service to
others is nowhere so well expressed as it is in his own
explanation of the Geat visit to the Danes. He and his
warriors would go to the aid of Hrothgar because ". . . there
is need of men."

To an uninformed reader Beowulf himself may seem
naive, innocent, simplistically eager for praise. But he is in
that one heroic gesture the best that the warrior class had to
offer, and he can even be argued to be one of the greatest
warriors in all of literature. His single-minded quest for glory
and praise, for *lof,* if you will, through valorous service (early
in the poem to Hrothgar and later, as king, to his own
people) is an example of what a man did when he was at his
finest, to live in service was to live supremely, and to die in
battle was to achieve glory forever. His generosity in
warring with all three monsters in the poem is a tribute to the

intensity of his belief in this Germanic concept of service. He correctly carries the ideal through to the last few moments of his life. Even as he lies dying he wishes one quick look at the riches that he has so dearly won for his people, breathes his last as he gives thanks for the opportunity to have done so. He was aware that in the end nothing endures but the reputation of a man.

The early audience of the poem was aware of that as well. They understood both the meaning and the depth of his generosity as essentially heroic in nature.

This giving of riches to his retainers and to his people (an idea that exists even today as the dispensing of medals for valorous duty), is simply the fulfilling of his warrants as a leader. It is pagan generosity at its best and it permeates the poem.

And no gift for service to the *comitatus* could be more prized by a warrior than that of armor or weapons. Such gifts were the signature of the most generous of leaders to the dearest of followers. Simply enough, there was not that much of it to go around. Armor was in fact so esteemed that any significant piece had a history and reputation and was itself the subject of folk tales. The value of the gift of armor was mistaken by neither the king nor the warrior nor again by the contemporary audience of the poet. If you were peasant and were attacked by a warrior on horseback and in chain-mail and helmet who brandished a great sword as he thundered towards you, and if all you had to oppose him was a wooden hoe, you knew he was rich and you knew he meant business, and you had an immediate and awesome idea of what that armor could mean to a man who had chosen the military life. And what it could mean to a man who had none.

The heroes of BEOWULF and even the contemporary audience of the poem clearly lived in a warrior society. For the man who had even slight leisure there was not much to do over the long haul except eat and make war. In the evenings it was a wise thing to get inside out of the dark (where you could get hurt), feast heavily, and drink mead until sleep came. It was essentially a harsh world, and the men who peopled it were of necessity harsh also. The women of that time, the peace weavers, were at least as likely taken advantage of in real life as they were in the poem. If it was anybody's, it was a man's world.

The Christian touches that are found in BEOWULF are an intrusion into this harshness. The poet succeeds well in his embellishments, although the resultant direct and indirect references to Christianity woven into the poem generally amount to aphorisms and are nowhere so touching or heartfelt as the matter of the pagan warrior and the *comitatus*. And it is well to admit that. The Christianity in the poem is essentially an overlay. It is facile and talented, it may even be argued to improve the poem, may in fact be a patristic attempt to make the thing better relate to a changing world, but it is an overlay nonetheless.

The early audience of BEOWULF, those who knew the separate stories and then whatever versions which preceded the one we have, assuredly was not composed of Christians who had learned to endure the pagan content of the poem; they were still essentially pagans who were slowly accepting the tenets of Christianity, but only if its philosophy as presented was closely similar to the warrior ideal.

Gregory's admonition to Augustine to convert the Anglo Saxons slowly and by easy degrees was a splendid piece of advice. The Church Fathers knew the stubborn obstinacy of the average pagan mind. And they knew how to deal with it. One need only glance at the missionary art of today to see that the practice of converting pagans to Christianity by progressive minimal deviations from the prevalent social and religious institutions familiar to them has by no means died away.

In years far antecedent to the BEOWULF poem paintings exist which depict a militant Christ; He was a Christian Warrior far earlier than he was the Prince of Peace.

And so were his followers. Many early Christian heroes, in fact, were presented as paragons of warriors.

In Marmadonia, for example, Saint Andrew, facing his enemies, " . . . prayed in his heart, and quickly they were dead." In the less expedient centuries closer to our own, Andrew would have had to face and convert his enemies rather than so easily rid himself of them.

And in the convoluted discussions which abound concerning the organic extent of the Christian matter in

BEOWULF, there are few who ever deeply wished there were more of it. The BEOWULF poet, as a matter of fact, very likely was writing the version we have to Christian editorial order. We simply do not know. But for any critic to insist that the poem is *essentially* Christian suggests that the poet did not have the imagination or the skill to work the Christian elements present in BEOWULF into an already existing poem, or even poems, and smacks of a critic prone to convenient conclusions. It suggests, in fact, that creative writing is somehow a modern invention, denies that the first writers began by drawing pictures on cave walls thousands of years before even thinking of pounding on hollow logs.

Should we wish to indulge in outright fancy, why not suppose that somewhere in an obscure little church library tucked away in the southwest corner of England there just might be a more pristine version of the BEOWULF manuscript stashed away in a dust covered and long forgotten trunk, quietly waiting to be discovered. Now, there's a thought to make your secret pagan heart spirit rise up with joy.

THE POEM

* * * * * * * * *

Although non-scholarly readers of poetry in the main are more interested in what a poem says and the thoughts and emotions it evokes than they are in its structure, the mechanics of the poem and the words themselves of BEOWULF, as the work exists in Cotton MS Vitellius A XV, are nonetheless sufficiently removed from what even an educated reader is used to that a few words of explanation are in order.

The version of BEOWULF we have was written at least a thousand years ago in what is generally called Old English. It is a narrative poem some 3200 lines long. In each of these lines there is a pause in the approximate middle, the caesura, which separates the two half lines.

In general each half line has two stress points or accent beats, and quite often the sounds on two or three of these four beats per line alliterate. This phenomenon of Old English has received its share of attention by scholars apt at counting.

The action of the poem accounts for its overall structure. Roughly it is separated into two broad parts, the battles against Grendel and then Grendel's mother, and the battle against the dragon. Aside from these scenes, which at their best are splendid, much of the poem is composed of digressions and quick episodes, almost exclusively fabulous. The dialogue is highly dignified and stately.

Criticism is leveled at BEOWULF because of its loose structure, its discursive nature, its formalized speeches, its lack of steady narrative advance, and its great length. Such criticism withers, however, simply by examining what the poet is trying to achieve. The ambling nature of the poem, the digressions, the lack of surprise in the plot -- these are the tools of a great poet who is interested in producing *tone,* not story.

The stories themselves were already well known to even the uneducated audience of the poem. There were no surprises in BEOWULF. The listener would have to go elsewhere for new *what if* stories. Knowing the BEOWULF tales, he most certainly looked to the *scop* to strum away and sing at length of incidents in the lives of heroes who overcame the harsh environment, with the supernormal creatures in BEOWULF the personification of that environment. To that extent it is perfectly acceptable to suggest that Grendel represents the North Sea. Each of the monsters, in fact, represents an overwhelming obstacle to survival.

What the listener wanted over the course of an evening (or perhaps two evenings) was not just an action story but a story of mood and tone, one that not only related what happened, but why and how, and suggested at length the possibility of living in defiance of great odds.

It was the job of the *scop* to tell the tale with grace and dignity, and with a rich vocabulary and a complex syntax that would suggest the grand nature of the simple gesture of "hanging on . . . . "

The loose structure of BEOWULF, then, is one of the less notable things to a modern reader. What is most awesome about the poem concerns the stunning achievement of its massive tone. This tone is often described as elegiac, as a towering sadness in the face of a harsh *wyrd* (the Germanic concept of *fate* permeates the poem), as an elevated and stately archaism, as perseverance and endurance in the face of overwhelming odds, as a kind of heroic *ubi sunt.* All of these suggestions are true. However it is described, the tone is the entelechial force of the poem.

A large portion of the tone stems from the vocabulary of BEOWULF, and extensive work has been done to describe the complexity and richness of that vocabulary. Statistical studies abound which discuss the number of compound words in the poem, the number of words which deal with *fate, battle, death, honor,* and so on, and the high number of dictionary entries needed in a poem of only moderate length. The significance of the vocabulary of

BEOWULF should not be underestimated even by the casual reader.

To the early listener, hearing BEOWULF would be to luxuriate in the glories of the English language as well as to be captured by the subject matter. That is an attitude the average Englishman clearly would understand even today. To either listener the fact that BEOWULF took some four hours to hear to completion would make the poem seem far too short.

In this quest for tone, as well as vocabulary the poem makes frequent use of the *kenning,* the *litote,* and the *paraphrastic sentence.*

One of the more interesting of these figures, and one used heavily (in BEOWULF and in other Old English poems as well) is the *kenning.* Simply enough, it is the poetic use of several words to replace another, generally a noun. Thus "whale ways" is the ocean, "battle sweat" blood, "peace weaver" a woman, and so on. Some of these *kennings* are highly imaginative and evocative; they are nowhere in Old English poetry better than they are in BEOWULF.

The *litote* is a fairly rare figure of speech in which the meaning of a word is expressed by the reverse of its opposite. For example, a warrior of "no little size" would be gigantic. In BEOWULF the figure becomes understatement, tends to add to the wry, fatalistic presence in the piece.

The *paraphrastic sentence* in BEOWULF is its single most compelling structural phenomenon; at times the technique threatens to overwhelm the poem. But it is the most fascinating feature as well, when seen at its best a source of great joy. Simply put, it is the technique of paraphrase, the saying over and over, each time quite differently, of the matter of one of the half lines.

There are many other features, syntactical as well as structural, which in a longer discussion might be mentioned, and which in fact contribute to the tone of the poem. The only point necessary to be stressed here, however, is that the effect defines a poet of consummate skill. He makes it all look so easy. Of course it is not. Great art is not simple; it only gives, if it is at its best, the illusion of simplicity. Great art is in fact quite complex and at every stage intentional. And so it is with BEOWULF.

*　*　*

As he begins, the translator is forced to make certain assumptions about the task ahead. He must assume, for example, that the work in question is worth the effort of bringing a rough translation into final form, worth the year or more of steady work that he will invest in doing that and essentially nothing else, whether or not he is at the writing table. He must assume, when other translations exist, that he can get closer to the intent of the poet and closer to the words as they existed than others have. And most importantly, in this effort he must assume that he will be as uncreative as possible in an effort to keep his own work as unobtrusive as possible. These assumptions are especially difficult with BEOWULF. Because it is at once so near to

and so different from current English, it is particularly taxing
not to want to help the thing along so that every reader is
certain to see what the translator in his zest sees. In fact, in
some of the lesser of the existing translations there seems
to be the condescending inference, however, subtle, that
while the BEOWULF poet was skilled, work must be done
not only to translate but to improve the poem sufficiently to
make it palatable to a modern taste. That is an error. It is
the translator's job when dealing with the same language not
to find new words but only modern versions of the existing
words, and when compelled to, to supply only what is
absolutely necessary and only what is in general keeping
with the poet's intentions.

As to methodology, I have capitalized the first word
of each line, I have tried to retain the essential shape of the
poem, and I have retained the caesura. It seems to me that
retaining these attributes is the most suggestive and least
intrusive method of connoting the Old English poetic line.
Where the four beat line modernized naturally I have
retained that feature also, as well as the alliterative pattern.
I have tried never to force the alliteration of the poetry, nor
have I ever artificially fleshed out a line to enhance the
meaning, or to make it more "poetic." I take such an effort to
improve rather than to correctly modernize to be an insult to
the poet and to the poem. Where there was difficulty in
interpreting action or meaning (there are more than a few
passages which defy easy modernization), initially I tried to
keep the *scop* and the thrust of the poem in mind. What

might he have emphasized as he charged along, moving his body and his arms in a practiced and artful fashion? There were more than a few answers in that approach. Of one thing you may be certain -- the contemporaries of the BEOWULF poet had no difficulty in understanding the action and in figuring who was doing what to whom. They knew the stories and they knew the language, and they had the clear skills of the *scop* (the emphatic music of his harp, his intonations, his graceful body movement) to suggest action and meaning. In those few cases when there is no clear suggestion to help define meaning and action I ended up by reading about the crux, sampling the work of other translators, and then supposing.

I have used only several words that would not be immediately familiar to a modern reader -- *mere, scop, byrnie, corselet,* these and one or two others are words which some readers might recognize but not all; they are words so suggestive of the Germanic viewpoint in BEOWULF and add so much to the stately tone in the poem that to make them very modern seemed inappropriate. And indeed if BEOWULF was a poem which used archaic language to suggest the sad awareness of an even older time, it is fair to use some archaisms today to suggest that antiquity to a modern reader of the poem.

Most every translation of BEOWULF is accompanied by discursive prefatory matter in more or less generous detail which covers the art, structure, versification, diction, tone, audience, authorship, scribes, dating paganism,

Christianity, historical significance, and similar endless topics of the poem -- each translator judiciously accounting for the best that has been thought and said, while carefully attempting some new perspective or insight as justification for his own efforts. Much of this critical palaver is supposition, the more or less logical result of historical inference or " . . . textual evidence." And most of it, assuredly, would bring at the least a tolerant smile from the BEOWULF poet (or poets).

For the modern reader, however, the only *raison d'etre* of BEOWULF or any piece of literature is the fact that in the end and for whatever the reason, it still is or is not worth reading.

That is an issue, of course, that each of us will have to answer for himself.

Is it, in fact, a ripping good story? As well as story, does it have some suggestions as to how to endure in a less than perfect world? These are questions to be asked.

The answers lie deep within the value we place on sudden unexpected literary insights and those little epiphanies that explain life and make it tolerable and at the best of times even joyous. And for those who care enough to look closely, the answers are perfectly clear.

STORY LINE OF THE POEM

* *

(1-709)

The narrator rehearses the story of Scyld Scefing, a mythical Danish king, praising his war prowess, his goodness, and his fitness to rule. At his death Scyld Scefing is buried at sea. Hrothgar, also an excellent ruler, builds the great hall Heorot, and therein fulfills his warrants by giving great feasts and dispensing treasure to his loyal and joyous followers. Grendel, a fiendish monster in the shape of a man, cannot stand the happiness of the Danes, and in anger and malice he attacks Heorot one night, killing thirty warriors as they sleep in the hall after the drinking of beer. He repeats this hostility on the following night, and keeps up his attacks for some twelve years. Those who would escape the clutches of the fiend have long sought sleep in buildings farther off. Heorot stands empty and without celebration.

Hrothgar is consumed with anguish; he and his warriors and counselors are unable to find relief for Heorot.

Beowulf, the young kinsman of Hygelac the Geat and also his mightiest thane, hears of Grendel's malevolent deeds, and eager to secure glory (in the best of the Germanic heroic traditions), he vows to come to the aid of Hrothgar and the Danes. With fourteen warriors chosen for their superiority at battle, he sails to the land of the Danes. When they arrive, the guard of the coast challenges and questions them. He is immediately impressed by Beowulf's appearance and his speech of explanation, however, and eagerly he shows them the way to Heorot. Wulfgar, the king's herald and advisor, questions Beowulf once again as to the purpose of their visit, and Beowulf relates his wish to speak with Hrothgar. Wulfgar passes the message on to Hrothgar, who orders the warriors welcomed at Heorot. Beowulf enters the great hall, speaks with Hrothgar, and offers to cleanse Heorot single-handedly. A feast is ordered.

At the banquet, Unferth, a Danish courtier who has drunk too many beers, challenges Beowulf's courage and war skills by relating his version of Beowulf's swimming match with Breca. Beowulf vindicates his actions with the true story of the match, concluding that neither Unferth nor any Danish warrior represents a threat to Grendel, and he boasts that this night Grendel will know the worth of a Geat warrior. The feast continues as Beowulf vows to

Wealtheow, Horthgar's excellent wife, that he will defeat Grendel in combat.

Hrothgar, who leaves Heorot in the care of Beowulf, retires for the night; the Danes leave with him. Beowulf has resolved to fight Grendel without the use of weapons. All the Geats fall asleep save Beowulf, who, his anger and resolve growing, lies in wait for Grendel.

(710-1250)

Grendel, coming over the moors by cover of night, approaches the hall, thrusts open the door, quickly seizes the completely devours one of the Geats. He attacks Beowulf but is grasped by him (Beowulf has the strength of thirty men in the grip of one hand). There is a long and difficult battle; Beowulf finally manages to tear off Grendel's arm at the shoulder, the monster wailing an inhuman scream of pain. He escapes, leaving behind his hand, arm, and shoulder. He knows he is doomed.

The next morning many warriors follow the tracks of Grendel to his lair at the blood-stained mere. They return to court while a *scop* recites lays about Sigemond and Heremod.

Hrothgar comes to the steps of the hall to view the arm of Grendel and delivers a speech in praise of Beowulf. A great feast of celebration is prepared and enjoyed. Treasures are dispensed; appropriate gifts are given to Beowulf and his followers. After the banquet Hrothgar and his retinue and the Geats leave the hall, which is once again under Danish control.

(1251-2199)

Grendel's mother attacks Heorot that night, seeking revenge for the death of her son. She carries off the favorite thane of Hrothgar, Aeschere, as well as Grendel's arm. Beowulf is sent for when the attack is discovered.

Hrothgar appeals to Beowulf for help again, laments for Aeschere, promises great gifts if Beowulf will accept the challenge and is successful. He describes very vividly the horrible mere where the monsters abide. Beowulf counsels courage and reveals that he will go to the mere to fight the she-monster.

The Danes and the Geats travel through awesome countryside to the mere. Beowulf arms himself and dives into the lake, reaches the bottom, and battles with Grendel's mother. He kills the she-demon with a giant sword from the wall of her lair, and he cuts off Grendel's head. Above, Hrothgar and the Danes have ended their vigil and returned home, assuming that Beowulf has been slain. Beowulf finally surfaces, carrying with him Grendel's head and the hilt of the marvelous sword. He and his band return to Heorot victorious, carrying the hilt and the head of Grendel into the hall.

Long speeches are made by both Beowulf and Hrothgar. There is another feast, and then all find needed rest. After more long speeches the next morning, the Geats begin the journey home. Arriving at his uncle Hygelac's court, Beowulf narrates the whole of his adventure and relates a Danish political involvement with Hrothgar, in which his daughter Freawaru is betrothed to Ingeld. Beowulf generously shares his gifts with Hygelac and his wife Hygd. He settles in Geatland, where he is honored and beloved by the king.

(2200-2820)

Beowulf comes to the kingdom after the deaths of Hygelac and Heardred. He rules for fifty years. When the treasure hoard of a dragon is robbed by a fugitive, the dragon seeks revenge and begins to lay waste to the countryside.

Beowulf resolves to destroy the dragon. He has an iron shield built, knowing that a wooden one would be useless against the fire of the dragon. He will fight the dragon alone. He delivers a long speech, recounting his achievements. He bids farewell to the eleven warriors who have accompanied him to the barrow of the dragon.

Beowulf challenges the dragon but is overwhelmed by the fumes and the heat. Wiglaf alone of the warriors comes to his aid. He stabs the dragon in the soft underbelly, and Beowulf finishes off the dragon with a knife. But Beowulf himself has received a fatal wound. Wiglaf tends to Beowulf, and then yields to Beowulf's wish to see some of the treasure the two men have won. Beowulf is thankful that he has secured the treasure for his people, asks that a mound be built on the headland to commemorate him, and dies.

(2821-3136)

Wiglaf rebukes the warriors who fled, sends on a messenger to announce Beowulf's death. Death and dire things are predicted by the messenger. The Geats return to the scene of the fight, push the dragon's body into the sea, carry out the remaining treasure, and take Beowulf's body to the chosen site.

(3137-3182)

A great funeral pyre is built. Beowulf's body is burned, and a royal mound is built to forever remind all who see it of the great warrior's worth. Twelve warriors ride round the barrow, singing of the strength, the glory, the kindness, and the fame of their fallen lord.

BEOWULF

* * * * * * * * *

True it is, we have   heard of the splendor
Of the Danish kings   in days now long past.
What glorious deeds   those heroes performed.
       Often Scyld Scefing   deprived of their mead-halls
The warrior enemies,   many peoples, many times.
He terrified warriors,   he who before as a youth
Had begun his days destitute.   He awaited his time,
Grew under the clouds,   then earned honor and riches
Until those of all lands,   all the neighboring peoples,
10   Heard of his deeds   and sent him tributes
Over the whale-ways.   There was a king!
A son was   afterwards born,
A youth for his court.   God sent him
To the people as consolation   for the terrible distress
He saw they had suffered   in lacking a leader
For so long a time.   The Lord of Life,
The Keeper of Heaven   gave worldly honor to him.
This son of Scyld,   Beowulf, was renowned.

His glory spread wide   in Scandinavia.

20   So should a young man   strive to do good,
Give gifts costly and splendid   from his father's largesse,
So that in turn   his companions
In his age will stand by him,   and his people remain
When warfare comes.   In any nation
A man will prosper   if his deeds are lofty.

Scyld then went   to the Lord's protection.
He went forthrightly   when his time had come.
They bore him out,   his cherished companions,
To the surge of the sea,   as he had directed

30   When he had use of words,   this lord of the Scyldings,
Beloved prince of the land   who so long had held rule.
There at the harbor stood   the ring-prowed ship,
Ice covered, yet ready,   vessel fit for a king.
They laid him then,   this giver of rings,
Beloved of the people,   in the depths of the ship,
Splendid by the mast.   Many treasures were there,
Precious ornaments brought   from far distant lands.
Never have I heard   of a comelier ship,
So wrought with armor,   with battle-gear,

40   With swords and with byrnies.   In those depths lay
A wealth of treasures   that would journey with him
In the grip of the flood   to places afar.
By no means the less,   these heart-given gifts,
These treasures of the people,   than those given
To him at his birth,   when he was sent forth
Over the waves,   alone, but a child.
Next they placed   a golden banner above him,
High over his head.   They let the water take him then,
Gave him to the ocean.   Mournful in spirit

50 They endured that sorrow. Man cannot know,

   To say but the truth, neither counselor nor warrior

   Under the heavens, where that load was taken.

     Then in that region Beowulf of the Scyldings,

   Beloved king of his people, ruled a long time --

   His father gone elsewhere, his chief from the earth.

   People knew of him! -- until afterwards was born to him

   Lofty Healfdene, who ancient and battle-fierce

   While he lived, held those glorious Scyldings.

   And then four children all counted

60 Were born into his world, princes of humankind,

   Heorogar and Hrothgar, and good Halga --

   I heard that (. . . .) who was Onela's queen,

   Beloved mistress of that war-grim Swede.

     And then to Hrothgar, high-minded in battle,

   Were war victories bestowed, such that his men

   Obeyed him eagerly, and their numbers increased

   To a great band of retainers. It came to him then

   That he would order a great hall building,

   A better mead-hall be built by men

70 Than ever remembered by the peoples of earth.

   And within he would portion out gifts

   To the young and the old, God's bounty to him,

   Save only the public lands and the lives of his men.

   Then, as I have heard widely, a multitude of peoples

   From far over the earth were ordered to the work,

   To adorn that folk-place. Nor was it long

   As time is perceived before it was finished,

   That greatest of buildings. He called it Heorot,

   He whose words held wide command.

80 He kept his warrants; he dealt out rings,

And gave treasure at banquet.   And the hall towered high,
Lofty, wide-gabled.   Yet harsh flames were to come,
The ill will of fire.   Nor would it be long
Before the clashing of swords   between father and son-in-law
Should rise up,   bespeaking the hate of one for the other.
      Then an evil demon   endured distress;
He suffered sorrow   in darkness,
As day after day   he heard the rejoicing
That was loud in the hall.   There the harp sounded,
90   There the sweet song of the scop.   It was told by him
Who could sing of the ages   of the beginnings of man,
Told that the Almighty   had fashioned the earth,
This beautiful place,   had it surrounded by water,
And triumphantly set   both the sun and the moon
As beacons of light   for dwellers on earth.
He adorned the earth   and all of its regions
With limbs and with leaves,   and He gave life itself
To each moving,   to each living thing.
      So then the retainers   lived on in joys,
100   Happy to a man,   until this fiend from hell began,
This wasteland roamer,   to perform wicked deeds.
Grendel it was,   the name of this demon.
He who held the moors,   the fens his stronghold,
He was renowned   among the race of monsters.
The unhappy creature   guarded that place
After the Creator   had condemned him
With the race of Cain.   The Eternal Lord
Avenged that killing,   the slaying of Abel.
No joy in that battle,   for because of his wickedness
110   God drove Cain far   from the realm of mankind.
Then all of the brood   of evil was born,

Giants and elves   and malignant spirits,

Such monsters   as had fought with God

For uncountable years.   But He made them pay dearly for it.

      He went then to seek out,   when night had come,

That highest of houses,   to see how the Danes

Had settled in it   after the drinking of beer.

 In it he found   a band of heroes

Asleep after banquet;   they knew neither sorrow

120   Nor the misery of men.   The evil creature,

Grim and greedy,   was ready at once --

Fierce was that fiend --   and from their rest seized

Thirty sleeping thanes,   and as quickly he left,

Exulting in his spoils,   to get to his home,

To find then his lair,   with the glut of his kill.

Then just before dawn   and the break of day

The war-strength of Grendel   was seen by the men.

Where feasting had been   weeping rose up,

And great morning keens.   The stately king,

130   That best of leaders,   sat unhappily,

Suffering mightily,   consumed by sorrow for his men,

As they all stared   at the loathsome track

Of the accursed demon.   That strife was too long,

Too hostile, too lasting.   Nor was it longer

Than a single night   before the fiend came again

And murdered anew.   And he took glee

In his loathsome hostility   -- he loved his deeds.

Soon there were a great number   who for themselves

Then sought rest   in buildings further away,

140   Bedded far from the hall,   when they came to know,

When they truly came to see   through clear signs,

Of his hate for the hall thanes.   Who would escape the fiend

Took himself further off   to a safer distance.

And so he ruled   and fought against right,

Alone against all,   until it stood idle,

That best of houses.   The while was great,

Twelve winter's time,   that the lord of the Scyldings

Suffered affliction,   endured each grief

And sorrow that came.   Then men and their offspring too,

150   Came clearly to know,   had it made manifest

Through mournful recountings,   that Grendel fought

So long against Hrothgar;   enforcing enmity,

Wicked deeds, hostile acts,   continually fighting

For time beyond telling.   And no peace would he have

With any man   of the host of the Danes,

Nor stop the malignance,   nor settle with riches.

Nor was there a counselor   could hope to think

Of glorious relief   from the hand of the slayer.

But the hideous monster,   the dark shadow of death,

160   Kept at his harassment,   hovered, and ambushed

Trained retainer and youth.   He ruled the moors

In darkness constant;   men knew not whither

Such hell-wise demons   might roam.

        So this enemy of mankind,   this terrible solitary one,

Often inflicted   loathsome crimes

And terrible humiliations.   Heorot he held,

That richest of halls,   in the black of the night.

The fiend could not know   the throne's great gifts,

The munificence of God,   nor did he care.

170   That strife was a misery   to the lord of the Scyldings,

A great ache to his heart.   Many of his best

Often sat in high council   and spoke at great length

Of what the brave had at hand,   how best the strong-minded,

Could deal   with the fiendish horror.

For a time they went   to the heathen temple,

Gave honor to idols,   and prayed with clear words

For the soul-slayer himself   to give help to them

Against this distress.   Such was their custom,

Such the heathen hope.   Hell they remembered,

180   Hell in their minds.   God they knew not,

Nor the deeds of the Judge.   They knew not the Lord God,

The Prince of Heaven.   The Ruler of Glory

They neither praised nor knew.   Woe comes to him who

Through violence terrible,   condemns his soul

To the fire's embrace,   nor solace expects,

Nor a whit reforms.   And well for him

Who at the day of his death   goes to the Lord,

To the Father with outstretched arms,   to ask for peace.

So the daily sorrow   of Healfdene's son

190   Continually festered,   nor could that wise warrior

Turn the trouble aside;   when the cruelest distress,

The greatest night evil,   came to the people --

That fight was too long,   too hostile, too lasting.

        Then at his home   Hygelac's thane,

The best among the Geats,   heard of Grendel's deeds.

He was mankind's best hope,   the greatest in might

In the days   of this life;

He was noble and lofty.   He ordered a ship

Be made ready,   said he would go to seek

200   The good king,   that famous prince,

Far over the ocean,   because there was need of men.

In that great gesture   his tried retainers

Did not fault him;   they urged on the strong warrior,

And because they loved him,   they sought good signs.

This good man   chose then his warriors,

The bravest of the brave   that he could find

From among the Geats.   And fifteen all told

Sought out the ship;   the man, sea-skilled,

Along the seashore   guided them to it.

210   Before many days   the craft was on the waves,

Moored under the cliffs.   Eager, the warriors

Mounted the prow   -- the sea currents swirled,

Mingled water and sand;   the soldiers,

Adorned with armor,   bore bright trappings

Into the bosom of the ship.   The men pushed out,

Men in a ready ship   on a wished-for journey.

The foamy-necked vessel,   most like a bird,

Slid then over the sea,   thrust on by the winds,

Until after a time   on the second day

220   The curve-prowed ship   had gone far enough

So that the voyaging warriors   caught sight of land,

Saw sea-cliffs shining;   steep they were,

On a great craggy shore.   Then was the ship safe,

The voyage at its end.   The men of the Weders

With great haste   climbed down to the shore

And secured the ship;   their shirts of mail,

Brave war-dress rattled.   They thanked God

Because He had kept them   safe in their passage.

From the high cliff   the Scylding protector,

230   He who had the charge   of holding the shore,

Saw borne over the gangway   shining shields,

Bright armor ready.   Curiosity broke over him;

He wanted to know   just who the men were.

Down then to the shore   he went on horseback,

Hrothgar's retainer,   brandishing might,

Splendid spear in his hands,   and commanded, formal his

speech:

"Who be you,   armed warriors,

Protected with mail,   who in this high ship

Over the sea-roads   are come to this place

240   From over the water?   In truth, for long I have been

The guard of the coast,   have held watch by this sea,

So that no enemy   can come to us in ships,

To harm or to plunder   in the land of the Danes.

Never more openly   have shield bearing warriors

Here landed,   yet you have no permission

From our own warriors,   nor do you have

Kinsman's agreement.   Never have I seen

A greater man anywhere   than one of you seems,

So honored with weapons   and splendid in armor.

250   This is no ordinary retainer,   unless he belies his appearance

And great battle-trappings.   Now I will

Know your homeland   before you leave

To travel inward   like deceitful spies

On Danish land.   Now, you strangers,

You seafarers,   listen; hear my clear thought:

Haste is best   -- delay not;

Make known now   from whence you are come."

The chief among them   gave him answer,

The leader of that group   unlocked his words:

260   "We are men   of the Geatish people,

And the hearth companions   of Hygelac.

My father   was well known to all people,

A noble chief,   Ecgtheow his name.

He lived many winters   before he departed,

Old in his years.   Every man of wisdom now

Over all of the earth   remembers him easily.
For the best of reasons   we have come to see
Your lord,   Healfdene's son,
Protector of his people.   You must council us!

270   We have come to your leader,   the Danish king,
On a great errand,   nor shall it stay a mystery
If I have my way.   You know full well,
If things are   as we have heard tell,
That a mysterious malignance,   an enemy unknown,
Shows to the Scyldings   in the dark of night
And in the worst of ways   forbidding afflictions,
Humiliations, slaughters.   I wish, for lofty reasons,
To give council to Hrothgar,   to offer him help --
How he, wise and good,   might overpower that fiend,

280   If reversal is ever   to be his due,
If cure is to come   for that evil distress,
And the heat of sorrow   is to become more cool.
Else always   shall he endure affliction
And baleful woe,   as long as still stands
On the lofty seat   that best of houses."

      The Watchman spoke,   astride his horse,
The courageous retainer: "Each wise shield-warrior
Must decide for himself,   must see the distinction
Between words and deeds,   if he thinks at all.

290   You have said that   you are a troop
Committed to the Scylding king.   Go forth then bearing
Both weapons and armor;   I myself will show you!
And as well shall I order   my troop of retainers
Against any enemy   to guard your ship
So newly made;   that ship now moored
They will hold with honor,   until again it carries,

The curved-prow vessel,   this beloved troop,

Over the sea-streams,   to the land of the Weders,

Such of these who   have acted bravely

300   And safely passed   through the storm of battle."

They left then to go --   the ship remained still,

That ample ship   rested on its moorings,

Fast at anchor.   Boar heads glittered

Over helmets   decorated with gold,

Ornamented, fire-hardened,   -- protecting life

In these fierce, warlike minds.   The men hastened out,

Marching together,   until they caught sight of

The timbered hall,   gold covered and splendid,

That most famous   of buildings

310   Under the heavens.   The splendor of it spread

Over many lands.   There the king dwelt!

The battle-warrior,   resplendent he was,

Told how the troop might   come most directly

To that hall of great thanes.   Through the retainers

He turned his horse,   and then said back to them:

"Time is for me to go. May the Father Omnipotent,

With great grace,   keep your

Journey safe!   I at the shore

Will maintain the watch   against hostile foes."

320   The street was stone-paved,   the way clear

For the band of men.   War corselets shone,

Hardened, hand wrought,   bright ringed-iron

Clanging war-sounds,   when first to the hall

In their war-ready armor   they came marching.

The sea-weary warriors put down   their great shields,

Ornamented, invincible,   against the wall of that building,

And then sat at bench;   -- their coats of mail rang,

The armor of warriors.   The seafarers' weapons,
Their ashen spears,   gray-tipped,
330   Stood ready close by;   this iron-clad troop
Was honored with weapons.

                                Then a high-spirited hero there,
Asked the warriors   from whence they had come:
"Who sends you here,   with these gray shirts of mail
This lot of spears,   these visored helmets,
And these splendid shields?   I am Hrothgar's
Herald and advisor.   Never have I seen
So many strangers   so brave in spirit.
Not to seek exile,   but I hope in daring,
In greatness of heart   have you sought out Hrothgar."
340   To him the strong one   the daring man of the Geats,
Brave in his mind,   gave answer;
Spoke thus to him: "We are Hygelac's
Hall companions.   Beowulf is my name.
I will speak   to your chief,
To your glorious leader,   the son of Healfdene,
Of my errand   -- if he who is good
Will grant to us   that we might speak with him."
Wulfgar spoke,   he who was a Vandals man;
His spirit,   wise and valorous
350   Was known to many: "I will ask
The lord of the Scyldings,   the Dane of Danes,
Giver of rings,   and illustrious prince,
About your journey   as you request,
And will quickly relate   as answer to you,
What the famed prince   thinks to say in return."

                                He turned at once then   to where Hrothgar sat,
Aged and hoary   among his troop of retainers;

Then that strong one went   until he faced

The Danish ruler,   as he knew was correct.

360   Wulfgar spoke   to his friendly lord:

"To us have traveled,   have come from afar

Over the ocean's realms,   men of the Geats.

The chief   of these warriors

Is called Beowulf.   They give petition

My lord, that they   might speak,

Might exchange words with you.   Do not give refusal

As an answer,   gracious Hrothgar.

In their war-gear   they appear worthy

Of consideration as heroes: indeed, the chief

370   Who leads these warriors   seems splendid."

           Hrothgar spoke,   protector of the Scyldings;

"I knew him   when he was but a boy;

His father was old,   Ecgtheow he was called --

Hrethel of the Geats   gave to him

His only daughter in marriage;   now is his son

Come here in strength   seeking a trusted friend.

As well is it said   by our seafarers,

Who carried my gifts   to the Geats

As a token of thanks,   that this brave battle warrior

380   Has the strength   of thirty men

In the grip of one hand.   The Holy Lord

In His kindness   has sent him to us,

To the Danes   -- that is my hope --

Against the terror of Grendel.   To this good man

Because of his daring   shall I tender treasures.

Act now in haste;   call him to come,

To look upon my band of warriors   here gathered together.

Say to them this thought,   that they are welcome

To the Danish people."   [Wulfgar then went
390   To the door of the hall]   and said from within:
"To you I am ordered   by my victorious lord,
The king of the Danes,   to say that he knows of your lineage,
And you who have come   from over the billowing seas,
Brave-minded warriors,   are welcome here.
Now you may go   in your war garments
And wearing your helmets   to see Hrothgar;
Allow your battle shields   and your great ashen spears
To remain where they are,   until words end between you."
            The powerful one then rose   and all of his men,
400   Splendid troop of thanes;   some remained there
To guard the war gear   as the brave one commanded.
They hastened together,   the leader before them,
Under Heorot's roof.   The warrior went in,
Brave in his helmet,   until he stood at the hearth.
Beowulf spoke   -- his coat of mail shone,
Linked armored net,   skill of the smith:
"Health to you, Hrothgar!   I am Hygelac's
Kinsman and young retainer.   I have undertaken
Many mighty deeds in my youth.   To me in my country
410   Was Grendel's story   made perfectly clear;
Sea travelers have said   that this greatest of halls,
This best of buildings,   stands idle and useless
For warrior's delight   when darkness comes,
After the light of the sun   has been lost.
Then I was advised   by the best of my people,
The greatest   of hall counselors,
That I should seek you out,   chief Hrothgar,
For well do they know   the depths of my strength.
They themselves looked on   when I came from battle,

420	With blood shed by my enemies, where I took five hostage,
	Destroyed giants, and on the waves slew
	Water monsters by night, swam in severe distress,
	Avenged the Weder ills, crushed the hostile ones --
	They courted their troubles. And now against Grendel,
	Against that wretch, alone I shall carry out
	Revenge against the demon. Prince of the Scyldings,
	Chief of the Danes, I ask you now
	That you grant this single petition;
	Protector of warriors, friend to the people,
430	Refuse me not. Now that I have come so far,
	Let myself alone and my troop of retainers,
	Bravest of warriors, purge Heorot.
	Also, I have heard that this monster
	In recklessness cares not for weapons.
	Let me forsake them also -- and then Hygelac,
	My lord, may keep thoughts of me
	Without sword or great bossed-shield,
	Yellow war-weapon in battle -- but I with my hands
	Will grapple the enemy and fight for life,
440	Hated against hating; and resignation shall be
	To the judgment of God whom death shall take.
	I expect the monster if he gains control
	In the battle-hall will fearlessly feast
	On the Geatish troops, as he so often has done
	On the men of the Danes. Never shall you have need
	My head to bury, but he will have me
	Covered with gore, blood-stained in death,
	Blood-battle slain, as he means to devour me,
	To gorge himself, alone and ruthless,
450	Staining his moor-haven. And no need shall you have

To care for my body,   nor to lament long in sorrow.
Send on to Hygelac,   if the battle takes me,
This best of war-garments   defending my breast,
This greatest of byrnies: it is Hrethel's heirloom,
And was fashioned by Wayland.   Fate goes as it pleases."
        Hrothgar spoke,   protector of the Scyldings:
"For deeds we have done   and out of kindness
You have sought us out,   my friend Beowulf.
Your father in fighting   brought the worst of feuds.

460   He slew Heatholaf   with his own hands
Among the Wylfings;   then the Weders
In terror of war   dared not shelter him,
And so he sought out   the Scylding people,
Came over the rolling ocean   to the Danes.
It was then I first led   the Danish folk,
And in my youth held   the glittering kingdom,
Alive with great warriors;   Heorogar was then dead,
My older brother,   dead;
Son of Healfdene   -- and better than I.

470   Afterwards the feud   I settled with riches,
I sent to the Wylfings,   over the back of the water,
Ancient treasures;   he swore me oaths.
It sorrows me now   to the depths of my spirit
To say to any man   what Grendel has done --
What humiliations in Heorot,   with his hateful thoughts
And his dreadful attacks.   My hall troop,
My band of warriors is diminished,   swept away by the fate
Of Grendel's terror.   So easily might God
Separate the mad demon   from his horrible deeds!

480   Full often my warriors,   drunk with beer,
Boasted   into their ale cups

That they would wait   in the beer hall
To do battle with Grendel   with swords of terror.
Then was this mead-hall   at morning time,
This splendid hall,   drenched with blood;
The benches by light of day   were wet with gore,
The hall stained red.   I had then fewer to trust,
Those dear retainers,   for death took them.
Sit now to a feast,   and loosen your thoughts
490   Of the glories you know,   as you see fit."
        Then for the Geats   gathered together
In the beer hall,   a bench was cleared.
There the strong-minded   went to sit,
Proud in their might.   A thane attended them,
Bore in his hands   a hand-wrought ale cup,
And poured clear mead.   The scop sang as he might;
There was brightness in Heorot,   bliss of warriors,
Great retainers all --   Danish and Weders.
        Unferth spoke,   he was Ecglaf's son,
500   Who sat at the feet of   the Scylding king.
He started a quarrel --   Beowulf's journey,
The high-spirited seafarer,   was a vexation to him.
He wanted it such   that no other man
On this earth   might achieve more glorious deeds
Under the clouds   than he himself:
"Are you the Beowulf   who contended against Breca,
On the great sea   in a swimming match?
Where you both in pride   made a trial of the water
And for foolhardiness   ventured your lives
510   In deepest water?   There was no man,
Neither friendly nor hostile,   who might dissuade you
From that sorrowful journey   when you swam so hard.

There you the sea-streams   enfolded into your arms,

Crossed over the sea-paths,   flung your hands

In gliding over the ocean --   the ocean waves surged,

The winter's flood.   In the watery throes

You labored for seven nights;   he overcame you at swimming,

Had the more might.   On the last morning

The waves carried him up   to the Norwegian shore.

520   He sought out then   his own native land;

Beloved he was   in the land of the Brondings,

So fair a stronghold,   where he had followers,

And fortress, and treasure.   The truth went against you;

The son of Beanstan   fulfilled his boast.

And so I expect that you   can look to the worst,

No matter your faring   in every battle so far,

Grim weapon-clash,   if you take Grendel's dare

And await his coming   in an all night hall-watch."

        Beowulf spoke,   Ecgtheow's son:

530   "True, my friend Unferth,   a great many things

Because of much beer,   have you said about Breca,

Have you said about his side.   The truth, I maintain,

Is that I had more   of strength in the sea,

Struggled greater against waves,   than any other man.

Being but boys,   and boasting so

-- We both at the time   were hardly grown --

We vowed that   we would venture out

Into the vast ocean,   and we did as we said.

We had naked swords,   hard-iron in our hands;

540   As we swam out   we thought to protect ourselves

Against the whale.   Not a whit of distance

In the waves of the ocean   could he swim from me,

Nor could he swim faster;   neither would I leave him.

So we together   were in the sea
For five night's time;   the waves drove us apart then,
The surging of the water,   in weather most cold
And darkness growing,   with the north winds
Battle-grim against us,   and savage the waves.
The sea-fishes were   roused and angered;
550   Then my coat of mail,   strong and hand-locked,
Woven war-garment   adorned with gold,
Gave me protection   against the hostile ones
As it covered my breast.   There a loathsome enemy,
Grim and grasping,   took me to the bottom,
There held me fast.   Yet it was granted to me
That I destroy the monster   with the point of my sword,
Strong war-weapon;   in the storm of battle I slew
The mighty sea-beast   with my own hands.

          Again and again   the loathsome spoilers
560   Threatened me severely.   I served them well
With my beloved sword,   just as was fitting.
By no means had they   their fill of joy,
These wicked destroyers   that would devour me
As they sat around in banquet   near the deep sea-bottom;
But in the morning,   battered with sword wounds,
Strewn on the sand along the shore,   they lay dead --
Killed by my blade.   And so never again
Around the deep waterway   might they hinder
The seafarer's passage.   Light came from the east,
570   God's bright beacon;   the sea calmed,
So that I caught sight   of sea headlands,
And wind-blown cliffs.   Fate often protects
The undoomed man   when his courage is strong!
Just so, it was my lot   that I slew with my sword

Nine sea monsters.   I have never heard
Under the reaches of heaven,   of a harder night-fight,
Or on the water-stream   of a man more wretched;
Yet I passed safely   through that hostile trip,
Weary from the journey.   Then the sea carried me
580   Over the flood currents   and the surging waters
To the land of the Finns.   Not once have I heard
That you ever   were in such a match,
Or dealt such sword-terror.   Neither Breca
Nor you either   to this day
Have fought so boldly,   have settled the battle
With blood-stained swords   -- I do not boast of this --
Although it is true   you slew your own brothers,
Your closest kinsmen;   and so in hell
Shall you endure damnation,   no matter your wit.
590   I say the truth to you,   son of Ecglaf,
Never would Grendel,   the hideous monster,
So many terrors   and humiliations in Heorot
Have handed your prince,   if your mind and your heart
Were so battle-fierce   as you yourself claim.
But he has come to know   that he need not fear
A horrible sword-storm   at the hands of your people,
Nor does he at all dread   the Scylding hero;
So he takes his toll,   and shows mercy to none
Of the Danish people.   He does it in glee.
600   He kills and he feasts,   and expects no resistance
From the Danish host.   But soon he will know,
Before many more hours,   Geatish strength and courage
As he finds it in battle.   Then, with the light of day,
At the dawn of tomorrow,   who wishes may fearlessly
Visit the mead-hall,   when the sun clothed in radiance

Shines out of the south   over the children of men."

        Then there was joy   to the giver of riches,

Gray haired and battle-wise;   the chief of the Danes,

Guardian of the people,   saw help coming,

610   Knew that in Beowulf   was steadfast purpose.

There was laughter of warriors,   din that was pleasure,

Words that were joy.   Wealhtheow came forward;

She was Hrothgar's queen.   Mindful of courtesies,

Gold-adorned, she greeted   the men in the hall,

And first gave the cup,   this excellent wife,

To the Danish   guardian of the treasures,

Beloved by his people,   and bade him pleasure

At this beer-drinking.   He received it in joy,

The feast and the hall-cup,   this victorious king.

620   The woman of the Helmings   then went around

To each retainer and youth   and poured out portions

Of the precious cup,   until in time it came to be

That the ring-adorned queen,   prospering in spirit,

Brought the mead-cup   in graciousness to Beowulf.

She greeted the Geat,   and she thanked God

In words that were wise   that she might now find joy

Because she could depend   on a hero's hand

For relief from the chaos.   He took the cup,

Fierce battle-warrior,   that Wealhtheow offered,

630   And then he said,   as he readied for battle;

Beowulf spoke,   the son of Ecgtheow:

"I resolved in my mind   when I set out to sea,

Cast off the sea-boat   with my troop of men,

That the desires   of your people

I would accomplish   else I would perish in battle,

Fast in the grip of the fiend.   I shall perform

Manly deeds of honor,   or else

In this mead-hall   come to my death."

The woman liked well   the sound of those words,

640   The Geat's battle-speech.   She went then, gold-adorned,

Noble queen of the Danes,   to sit by her lord.

And time was as it had been   before in that hall;

Strong words were spoken   by strong men within,

Joyous sounds of a victorious people,   until before long

The son of Healfdene   thought to find

His evening rest;   he knew that the monster

Against the high hall   had intended a scourge,

Through the light of that day,   the length of the sun.

Now it had grown dark,   and night over all,

650   The creatures of darkness   would come to glide,

Black under the clouds.   All there stood up.

He then turned   to the other warrior,

Hrothgar to Beowulf,   wished him luck

In the control of the wine-hall,   and said these words:

"Never before have I entrusted   to any living man,

When I had the use   of my hand and my shield,

The hall of the Danes.   I do so to you.

Take and guard now   this best of houses.

Remember glory,   show strength of purpose,

660   Keep watch against the hostile!   You will want for nothing

If this desperate charge   does not destroy you."

Then Hrothgar left him   with his band of heroes;

The prince of the Scyldings   moved out of the hall;

The war chief wished   to find Wealhtheow, his queen,

For a companion in sleep.   The King of Glory had

Appointed the hall guardian,   as warriors were told,

As a stand against Grendel;   he accepted special service

For the prince of the Danes,   to keep watch against the giant.

Indeed, the man of the Geats   eagerly trod forth

670   In high-spirited might   and the Grace of the Lord.

He undid then   his ringed byrnie,

Took off his helmet,   and gave his great sword,

Iron decorated, hard,   to the attendant,

Ordered him to keep   ready all of that war gear.

Then this good man,   Beowulf of the Geats,

Spoke fully his boast   before he went in to bed:

"I think myself no less   in martial vigor,

In warrior's skills,   than Grendel himself;

Therefore I will not   kill him with sword,

680   So deprive him of life,   although I easily might;

He knows nothing of those good skills   for use in killing,

Or of cutting with great sword,   although he has a name

For hostile deeds;   therefore this night

We shall forgo the use of swords,   if he be brave enough

For such a battle.   And then let the wise God,

The Holy Lord,   judge which of our hands

Might rise in glory,   as He thinks fit."

The great warrior then bent down,   let a pillow take

His hero's face,   and about him many

690   Brave sea-men   sank to rest in the hall.

Not one of them thought   that he from that hall

Would ever leave   to see his dear home,

Neither people nor noble-town   where he was raised,

Because each one knew   that too many warriors,

Great Danish retainers,   murderous death had carried off

From that wine-hall.   But the Lord gave to them,

To the men of the Geats,   consolation and support

And good fortune in war,   so that they overcame the enemy

Through the power of one,   overcame him completely,

700   Through just one alone.   In truth is it said,

That Almighty God   has ruled mankind

For time beyond telling.

                                    At black night came striding,

The walker in darkness.   The soldiers were sleeping --

Those who held guard   of the gabled hall --

All except one.   It was known to the men

That the hostile one   could not quickly

Drag the men into shadow   if God did not wish it.

The one lay awake,   his anger growing;

Enraged, he waited   for the desserts of the battle.

710   Then, from over the moors,   under the cover of mists,

Grendel came gliding.   He bore the wrath of God!

The evil ravager   intended to ensnare

Some one of mankind   in that highest of halls.

He advanced under clouds   so that easiest he

Might come to the wine hall,   that gold-adorned

Warrior hall.   Nor was it the first time

That he sought   Hrothgar's home.

But never before   in the days of his life

Found he a severer warrior   or a stronger hall thane!

720   He came then to the hall   on a warrior's journey

Devoid of joys.   The door, iron banded and firm

Immediately gave way   when he gave it hand-thrust.

The hostile one swung open   that mouth of the hall.

He was enraged!   Quickly after this,

Spiteful with anger,   the fiend trod

Across the shining floor.   From his eyes issued

An unholy light,   most like fire.

Many retainers   he saw in the hall,

A band of warriors   sleeping together,
730   Troop of young thanes.   His spirit exalted.
The horrid demon   intended to tear
Life from the body   of each one of them
Before the day came,   now that he saw
Hope of full feasting.   But by no means was he fated
To devour any more   of mankind
After that night. The mighty warrior,
The kinsman of Hygelac,   saw how the wicked ravager
Wished to proceed   in sudden attack.
Nor did the monster   think to delay,
740   But he quickly seized   at the first instant
A sleeping warrior;   tore him resistless,
Bit through bones,   drank hot blood,
Swallowed huge chunks,   and soon had
Completely consumed   the dead man,
Even his feet and his fingers.   He stepped in nearer.
With one hand he grabbed   the strong-hearted warrior
As he lay there,   and then he reached
Towards him with his other;   Beowulf seized that one
With his own intent,   and leaned up on his elbow.
750   The herder of evil   soon came to know
That he had never felt   on this earth
A greater hand grip   in any other man
Anywhere;   fear for his body
Grew in his mind.   Nor could he move!
He wanted to get away,   wished to flee to his lair,
To seek devil's company;   this hall-visit was different
From any before   in the days of his life.
The good warrior,   the kinsman of Hygelac,
Remembered his evening words;   he stood upright

760   And held him fast;   fingers strained;

The giant strove to escape;   the man kept with him.

The notorious one intended,   if he could manage,

To secure his freedom,   and in doing it

To find fen shelter   -- his own hand bettered

In that hostile hand-clamp.   Sad journey it was

For the ravaging enemy   when he made for Heorot.

The royal hall resounded;   to all the Danes,

To all castle dwellers,   to all of those brave ones,

To all men was terror.   Both fighters were fierce,

770   Both hall-guarders enraged.   The building thundered.

It was a great wonder   that the mead-hall withstood

The battle-brave fighters,   that it fell not to earth,

Fairest of buildings;   but it was fashioned,

Within and without   with strong bands of iron,

Fabricated with skill.   Many were the mead-benches,

Splendid with gold   that came away from their moorings,

So I have heard,   where the hostile ones fought.

It was never a thought   of the Scylding counselors

That any man   by any means possible

780   Could destroy   that high and bone-adorned hall,

Could wreck it with skill,   except that the heat of fire

Might consume it.   A noise rose up --

Awesome and startling --   and a terror unnamable

Swept over the Danes,   over each of them

Who by the wall   heard the anguished wail

Of the hideous song   of the enemy of God,

Song without victory;   hell's bondsman

Lamented his pain.   He held him fast,

He who was   the strongest in might

790   In the days   of this life.

The protector of heroes would not   for anything
Abandon the murderous visitor   while he yet breathed,
Nor did he think   that the demon might be of use
To anything that lived.   Then the warriors of Beowulf,
Their renowned swords   drawn in support
Were eager to defend   the life of their lord,
Of the famous prince,   if they but could.
They did not know,   when they were minded to fight,
To seek out his soul,   those brave-minded
800   Battle-warriors,   and thought to hack
From every side,   that not one war-sword,
Not the best of swords   from over the earth,
Could do any harm   to the malefactor;
He had cast spells   on each victory weapon,
On every sword.   His leaving this life,
From the days   of his time,
Was to be miserable,   and the alien spirit,
Under the control of fiends,   had far to go.
Then it was discovered   by him who earlier
810   Brought affliction of spirit   and hideous deeds
To all of mankind   -- he was a foe of God --
That his body   would not do as he wished,
For the kinsman of Hygelac,   the high spirited one,
Held him with one hand;   each to the other
Was hostile while living.   The horrid monster
Suffered a wound;   on his shoulder was
A rending of flesh;   sinews sprung,
Joints burst.   To Beowulf was granted
Glory in that battle;   Grendel, mortally wounded,
820   Had to flee from there   to the fen slopes,
Seeking friendless abode;   and he knew with no question

That the end of his life,   the number of his days,
Was at hand.   The will of all Danes had
Come to pass   at that bloody conflict.
He who had come from afar,   wise and strong-minded,
Had then cleansed   Hrothgar's hall,
Had rid it of hostility.   He rejoiced in his night-work,
In heroic deeds.   The Geatish man
Had fulfilled his boast   to the Danes,

830   Had remedied the distress,   the evil sorrow,
Which they all   before had long endured
And for sad necessity   had to suffer,
That greatest of afflictions.   It was clear enough,
When later the battle brave one   laid down the hand,
The arm, and the shoulder,   -- all together there,
Grendel's grasp --   under the spacious roof.

Then in the morning,   as I have heard it,
There were many warriors   who moved in the gift-hall,
Folk-chiefs who came   from far and near,

840   Some from distant regions,   to observe the wonder
Of the hostile demon's tracks.   No man
Who examined the footprints   of the vanquished one,
Saw how he, disheartened,   overcome in battle,
Doomed, was driven off --   and gazed at the blood trail
He left as he fled   to the lake of the water-things,
Could ever think sad   his parting from life.
There the water was   boiling in blood,
A horrid swirl of waves,   all mingled
Hot with gore and   battle-blood surged;

850   Doomed to die, he hid,   devoid of joy,
In his fen refuge,   where he lay down his life
And his heathen soul;   there hell took him.

Then again came   a host of old comrades
And many young warriors   in a joyous journey,
Full of high spirits,   riding back from the mere,
Warriors on white steeds.   Now was the fame
Of Beowulf related!   It was said over and over
That neither north nor south   over the earth
Between the two seas,   was anyone else
860   Under the sun   ever better
As a shield-bearer,   or more fit to rule.
Not for a second, however,   did they fault their friendly lord,
The gracious Hrothgar,   king without equal.
For a while the brave warriors   let their fallow mares
Fare in a contest,   let them frolic
Where the pathways   seemed the most fair,
Where the known way was pretty.   And then a king's thane,
A man drenched with glory   and skillful at tales,
Who remembered   a great many
870   Of the old sagas,   spoke now new words
That were coupled with truth;   the man again began
To speak in his wisdom   about Beowulf's venture,
And with skill to relate   the whole of the story,
Artfully choosing his words.   Then he related everything
He had heard   said about Sigemund,
About his valorous deeds,   much of it new to the hearer;
The son of Waels' strife,   his far flung journeys,
Which the children of men   knew not at all of,
Warrings and crimes   -- except for Fitela -- ;
880   When nephew wished   uncle spoke to him of such things --
Sigemund to Fitela,   because they were forever
Comrades together   at every kind of battle.
A great many giants   they had slain

With their swords.   Sigemund's fame spread

In glory resplendent   after he was dead.

In a brutal battle   he had killed the dragon,

Guardian of the hoard.   A prince's son,

He ventured alone   under the gray cliff,

An audacious deed   -- he was still without Fitela --

890   Yet it was his lot   that the sword thrust penetrated

The wondrous spirit   clear through to the wall --

Splendid sword it was --   and in that thrust the dragon perished.

The warrior had   brought about through high courage

That he might enjoy   the things of his choice

Of the ring-hoard;   he loaded his boat,

Bore to its bosom   bright treasures,

This son of Waels;   the dead serpent melted.

      He was the most famous   of all the adventurers;

Known in all nations   for valorous deeds,

900   This protector of warriors   -- and in it he thrived -- ,

After Heremod   was diminished in power,

In strength, and in courage.   When with the Jutes

He fell under the control of the fiends,   was misled in treachery,

And quickly came to his death.   Surging sorrows

Were too long a companion;   he became to his people,

To all of his followers,   too great a burden.

Many the wise man   in earlier times

Who often deplored   his strong-willed coming,

Had counted on him   for remedy of suffering,

910   Had felt that the son of the king   should prosper

And come to excellence   and control of the people,

And the treasures of the stronghold,   the riches of warriors,

In the land of the Scyldings.   The kinsman of Hygelac

To everyone there   and to all mankind,

Was the more pleasing as friend;   evil consumed the other.
　　　　For a while longer they competed   on the gravel
　　　　　　　　　　　　　　　　　　　　street,
Riding their horses.   By that time the morning sun
Was bright in the sky.   Many warriors then went,
Strong in their minds,   to that best of halls
920　　To gaze at the battle-wonder.   And the king himself
Came from his bedroom,   possessor of treasures,
Well known for excellence,   with a great company;
He approached in glory   near to the mead-hall,
With his queen at his side   and a host of women.
　　　　Hrothgar spoke   as he reached the hall,
Stood on the steps,   saw the gold-adorned
Towering roof   and Grendel's hand:
"For this sight,   let us give
Quick thanks to God!   I have suffered a host of hostilities
930　　At the hands of Grendel;   God forever works
Wonder after wonder,   our Guardian in Heaven.
It was not long ago   that I had
No hope of relief   for the days of my life,
Nor to receive remedy   when this best of houses
Stood blood-stained   and sword gory.
The woe reached   far into each of my counselors,
Who saw no hope   of ever finding
This stronghold of the people   defended against hostility,
Against demons, evil spirits.   But now a warrior,
940　　Through the power of God,   has accomplished the thing
Which we all   before could not do,
For all of our wisdom.   In truth, she may say,
Whoever the woman   who brought forth this man
To the race of men   -- if she still lives -- ,

That to her the God of Old   was gracious
In her child bearing.   Now, Beowulf,
The best of men,   I will take you to my heart,
Will love you as my son;   keep this new kinship,
Guard it forever.   You shall lack nothing
950 Of the joys of this world,   should I have them to give.
Full often for less   have I given reward,
Honoring with gifts   more lowly men,
Inferior at fighting.   You have yourself
Performed such things   that your fame will live
Forever and longer.   May the Lord reward
You with goodness   as He always has done!"
   Beowulf spoke,   the son of Ecgtheow:
"We did that valorous duty,   attended to that fight,
Daringly engaged   the dreadful foe's force
960 With great good will.   I wish most strongly
That you might have seen   the demon himself,
The fiend, killed   as he came here!
I thought to bind him   at once,
With iron clasps   in the bed of death,
So that he   in my hand-grip should be stayed
In death's torment,   unless his body might depart.
I could not;   it was not God's will
That his going be hindered.   I did not firmly hold him,
The deadly foe;   he was too powerful,
970 This fiend, in his escape.   However, he left his hand
To save his life;   behind him stayed
The arm and shoulder;   nor with that leaving
Did the wretched man   secure any solace.
Nor will the loathly spoiler   live any the longer,
Killed for his sinning;   but pain has come

With a grip sufficient,   has clasped him tightly
In baleful fetters;   there he must await
The great verdict   -- outlawed for wickedness -- ,
To see how the Glorious Lord   will judge him!"

980 Then the man was more silent,   the son of Ecglaf,
In his boasting speeches   about warlike deeds,
When the nobles   looked up towards the high roof
And examined the hand,   result of battle-warrior's craft,
The fingers of the fiend;   each one at the end,
Each hard nail   was most like steel.
The heathen hand-claw   was to the warriors
Baleful and frightening;   each man said
That not the best   of the best of swords
Would touch it,   would have harmed

990 That blood-stained battle hand   of the demon.
Then it was quickly ordered   that Heorot's interior
Be repaired and decorated;   many there were,
Men and women,   who worked at the wine-hall,
Fit hall for retainers.   Tapestries on the walls
Shimmered, adorned with gold,   and many wondrous sights
There were for each man   who cared to look.
That bright building   was heavily damaged
Everywhere inside,   in spite of its iron strapping.
Hinges were sprung;   the roof alone was not damaged,

1000 Was left whole,   when the demon of deeds
The hostile one,   left in his flight,
Despairing of life.   Nor be fate easy
To flee from   -- though who will may try -- ,
But each with a soul,   each of the children of men,
Every person on earth,   at the last will seek,
Through sad necessity,   the prepared place

Where his body,   bound in the grave,
Will sleep after banquet.

                             Then it was time and proper
That the son of Healfdene   went to the hall;

1010   The king himself   wished for the banquet.
I have never heard of   a larger company
Or a better behaved   than these with their treasurer-giver.
The glorious warriors   sat down at the mead-benches
And rejoiced at the feasting.   Hrothgar and Hrothulf,
Strong-minded warriors   and kinsmen,
Courteously drank   many mead cups
In the highest of halls.   Heorot within
Was filled with friends;   no treachery at all
Did the Scylding men   seem to have in their hearts.

1020   The son of Healfdene   gave then to Beowulf
A highly adorned   golden battle banner,
Victory's reward;   many watched
As a helmet and byrnie   and a most precious sword
Were handed to the warrior.   Beowulf drank
His cup in the hall;   he had no need of shame, there,
Before the warriors,   at the dispensing of treasures.
I have never heard of a   friendlier giving
By one man to another   across the ale bench
Of four such treasures   adorned in gold.

1030   The crown of the helmet   was bound with wires,
Ringed heavy outside   to protect the head,
So that the filed-sharp sword   in the storm of battle
Could do him no damage   if ever the shield-warrior
Found the need to go   against hostile enemies.
The protector of thanes   ordered eight horses
With golden bridles   drawn into the hall

Under the high roof; there one stood,

Its saddle adorned with war gear and treasures;

The saddle it was of the high king.

1040 When that son of Healfdene wished to make use

Of his sword's might, never was his known valor

Too little when the slain in battle were falling.

And then the prince of the Danes conferred possession

Of both to Beowulf, both horses and weapons;

And entreated him to use all wisely.

So, in the manner of men the famous ruler,

Hero guardian of treasures, repaid the storm of battle

With mares and with treasures said to be faultless

By any who wishes to speak with truth and right.

1050 Then still the lord of thanes gave treasures

To each one of the men at the mead-bench

Who made the sea voyage at the bidding of Beowulf --

Each was an heirloom -- and ordered gold to repay

For the one which Grendel before

In crime had killed; he would have taken more,

Except that the Wise God and the courage of the man

Had forbidden that fate. The Lord forever controls

All of mankind; He did and He does.

Therefore is understanding everywhere best,

1060 Foresight of the mind. Much must he live through,

Both of love and of hate, who for long here

In the days of strife would endure in the world!

     Songs there were and music together;

In the presence of Healfdene's battle-leader

The wood-harp was touched and tales were recited,

When Hrothgar's scop moved along the mead-bench

And related in hall-entertainment the story

Of the men of Finn -- how the sudden attack befell them,

How Hnaef of the Scyldings, the hero of the Danes,

1070 In a Frisian battle-field had to fall.

No need at all for Hildeburh to praise

The Jute's good faith; guiltless, she lost

Her loved ones at shield-play,

Both son and brother; fate took them down,

Ended by spears; there was a sad woman!

Not without cause did the daughter of Hoc

Bemoan fate's finality when morning came

And she saw the murdered men

Under the skies where she once had held

1080 All the world's delight. Warfare seized each

Of Finn's thanes, except a few only,

In the battle-field, so that he could not

Fight at all, could not war against Hengest,

Bring no conflict to the battle-survivors

Of that prince's thane; but they brought terms;

They cleared for them another mead-hall,

A hall and throne, and said that they

Might have half the control with the sons of the Jutes,

And each time at treasure giving

1090 The son of Folcwalda should honor the Danes

And present ornaments to the men of Hengest,

Even as often and just as willingly

As he honored his own Frisians with treasures,

With beaten gold, in the beer-hall.

Then they concluded on both sides

A strong compact of peace. Finn to Hengest

Stated his oaths boldly and bindingly,

Said that he would give honor to those survivors of war

On advice of his counselors,   that none of his men
1100   Were ever to break   that pledge in word or in deed;
Nor speaking in hate   might they ever utter,
Deprived of their leader,   that it was the slayer
Of their ring-giver they followed,   as they had to.
And if the Frisians,   in words outlandish,
Were to call up   the murderous hates,
Then the sharp sword-edge   would settle the thing.
The fire was made ready,   and golden things
Drawn from the hoard.   The greatest Scylding,
That best of warriors,   was readied for the fire.
1110   At that funeral pyre,   in front of them all,
Was the blood-stained mail-shirt,   and the golden boar-image,
Iron-hard boar helmet,   and many a good warrior,
Covered with wounds   -- these, slain in battle, fallen!
Hildeburh called then   for her own son
To be committed to the flames   at Hnaef's funeral pyre;
His body to burn,   to be laid to the fire
At his uncle's side.   The woman lamented,
Keened sorrow-songs.   The warrior was lifted;
The greatest of funeral pyres   climbed to the clouds,
1120   Roared before the mound.   Heads melted,
Flesh-wounds burst open,   body-blood splattered
From war-rents terrible.   Like a ravenous demon,
The fire took all   of those who had fallen
From both sides of battle;   their time had come!
        The warriors then left   without these friends,
Took themselves back,   returned to Friesland,
To cities and homes.   Hengest remained
Through the death-stained winter,   stayed with Finn,
Lacking a choice.   He thought of his land

1130   But he could not steer   his ring-prowed ship

In the driving seas.   The ocean-slashed storms

Raged with the winds;   winter took all

In bondage of ice.   In time spring came,

As it has always,   keeping the signals

Of times of the year,   glorious green

And sun-bright weather.   Winter was gone

And earth's bosom was fair.   The adventurer left then,

That guest at court;   full revenge for injury

Held his mind more   than the journey by sea,

1140   How he could harass   in a hostile meeting,

Remembering all   of the Jutish men.

So he did not disdain   the royal desire,

When Hunlafing   gave to his keeping

The battle sword,   that sword of swords,

An edge well known   to Jutish men.

And so to Finn   the bold-hearted,

Death came at home   in an angry attack

By cruel sword,   when Guthlaf and Oslaf

Spoke their sorrow   after the sea voyage,

1150   Blamed him for misery;   their restless hearts

Ached in their breasts.   Then was the hall reddened

With the blood of enemies,   and Finn himself was slain,

King of those troops.   His queen was taken.

The Scylding warriors   bore to their ship

All the possessions   of the king of that land;

Such treasure, too,   from that house of Finn --

Precious brooches, fine jewels.   Then over the ocean

With the splendid woman   to the Danes they traveled,

Brought her to her people.

                      The lay was sung,

1160   The gleeman's song.   Joy again arose,

        Clatter of the mead-bench grew;   cup-bearers gave wine

        From glorious vessels.   Then Wealhtheow came forth,

And went with golden crown,   to where the two good ones,

Nephew and uncle, were sitting;   at that time their peace held;

Each still faithful to the other.   As well Unferth the spokesman

Sat at the feet of the Scylding king;   every man there trusted

His spirit, his mind of worth,   however he had dealt

With his kinsmen before the sword-work.   Then spoke the woman of

                          the Scyldings:

        "Receive this cup,   my noble lord,

1170   Giver of rings!   Be you in joy,

        Gold-friend of men,   and speak to the Geats

        With softness in words,   as a man should!

        To these Geats be generous,   mindful to give

        Of what you now have   from near and far.

        My ears have heard   that as a son

        You would now think of this warrior.   Heorot is cleansed,

        This bright ring-hall.   Give him then while you might

        Earned riches and rewards,   but leave the rest to your men,

        To your people, to your kingdom,   when at last you must stand

1180   To the decree of fate.   Well do I know

        My gracious Hrothulf,   that he will hold in honor

        The young warriors,   if before him,

        Friend of the Scyldings,   you do leave the world;

        I expect that he with goods   will repay

        Our children   if he but remembers

        What things   in both delights and honor

        We did help him   when he was but a child."

        She went then to the bench   where her sons were,

        Hrethric and Hrothmund,   and the children of others,

1190   Youths there together;   there the good one sat,
        Beowulf of the Geats,   there by the two brothers.
               The cup was brought to him,   and twisted gold
        With good will presented to him,   two arm-ornaments,
        And corselets and rings,   and the grandest neck-piece
        Which ever was seen   on the face of the earth.
        Never have I under the heavens   ever heard of a better,
        From treasure hoard of warrior,   since Hama carried off
        To the bright city   the Brosing necklace,
1200   -- That brilliant and costly thing.   He fled from the treacheries
        Of Eormenric,   and chose eternal council.
        Hygelac of the Geats   next had the ring,
        Swerting's nephew,   from the time
        That his rule   protected the treasure,
        Held the battle-spoils;   trouble took him off
        When because of pride   he tempted fate
        In battle with the Frisians.   He took the treasures,
        Those precious stones,   over full waves,
        Prince of the people;   he fell under his shield.
1210   The body of the king   passed then into Frankish hands,
        With the coat of mail   and the great collar together;
        Ignoble the warriors   who plundered the fallen
        Geatish warriors   after the slaughter;
        Geats held but the ground of the dead.   The hall heard praise
                              of them!
        Wealtheow spoke,   said words before the company:
        "Enjoy this collar   dear Beowulf,
        Youth, and prosper;   delight in this corselet,
        Treasure of a people;   and flourish properly,
        Show yourself with skill.   And to these youths be
1220   Gentle in council!   I will remember you for it.

You have brought it about   that far and near
Forever and after   men will praise you --
Just as widely   as the sea flows,
As the winds are walled.   Then be you while living
Noble and blessed!   While you have life,
Get treasures!   Be you gentle
In deeds to my sons;   do so joyfully.
Here is each warrior   true to the others,
Gentle in spirit   and loyal to his lord;
1230   The thanes are united,   the people alert,
The retainers flush with drink,   and they do as I bid."

          She went then to her seat.   There was the best of
                                    banquets;
Warriors drank good wine.   They knew not their destiny,
Knew not grim fate   as it was to come
To many of the warriors   after evening fell,
And Hrothgar had gone   to his house,
Great ruler to rest.   Many the warrior
Who then guarded the hall   as they so often had done.
They cleared away the bench-floor;   it was spread over
1240   With beds and with cushions.   Some beer drinkers
Fell to hall-rest,   fated to die.
They set at their heads   their battle-shields,
Trusted bright armor;   there on the bench
Over those warriors   and easily visible,
The towering battle-helmets,   their ringed byrnies,
The magnificent spears.   Their custom was
That they always   were ready for warfare,
Both at home and in the field,   everyone and always
And on any occasion   that their war-leader

1250   Felt the need.   There was an excellent people!

                    (EXTRA SPACE)

               They sank into sleep.   Sorely did one pay

For his evening-rest,   as too often had happened before,

When Grendel   occupied the gold-hall

And did as he pleased,   until his end came

And he died for his sins.   It became evident,

Widely known to the men,   that an avenger still

Lived after the hostile one,   for all the time

After the carnage;   Grendel's mother,

That female monster,   bore in mind that misery;

1260   She who was forced to live   in that sorrowful water,

Streams cold beyond telling,   because Cain was

The first sword slayer,   took his own brother,

His kinsman through father.   He went then, guilty,

Marked in that murder,   to flee from man-joys

And inhabit the wastelands.   Then many damned spirits

Awoke to ravage,   -- Grendel was one;

A loathsome accursed foe   who found at Heorot

A man awake   and waiting for warfare;

There the monster   lay hold on him;

1270   However, he called up   the strength of his might,

His gem-like gift,   which God had given him,

And he trusted   to the mercy of God

For help and support;   he who overcame the fiend,

Handled the spirit of hell.   Then he went wretched,

Deprived of joys   to see his death-place,

This fiend of mankind.   And his mother then,

Ravenous and gloomy,   wished to go

On a perilous journey,   to avenge her son's death.

               She came then to Heorot,   where the ring-Danes slept

1280   Deep in that hall.   The warrior's lives

Were changed forever   when Grendel's mother

Passed into the hall.   The terror was less

Only so much   as is a woman's skill

In martial power   less than weaponed men

When finished swords,   forged by hammer-force,

Are adorned with blood,   boar-decorated helmets

Cut unopposed   with frightful strong edge.

Then in the hall   was heard the sword's-edge

Raised high over the benches,   and many the shield

1290   Grabbed by fierce hand;   forgotten in the horror

Were the ringed byrnies   and the bright boar-helmets.

The mother was frantic   to be out of there,

To save her life   when she was discovered.

Quickly she seized   one of the warriors

With an avenging hand,   and then she fled to her den.

He was to Hrothgar   the most loved of his advisors,

The best of retainers   between the two seas,

And a powerful shield-warrior;   she cut him down in sleep,

This glorious hero.   Beowulf was not there,

1300   The illustrious Geat;   he was elsewhere

Assigned to a hall   after the treasure-giving.

Panic in Heorot!   Gore-laden she had taken

That well-known hand;   sorrow was renewed,

Lamentations in the hall.   No exchange for the good

When both sides must pay   for the lives

Of their friends!

                 Then the aged king,

The gray-old warrior,   was troubled in spirit,

Knew in his sadness   that his chief thane was lifeless,

Realized this dearest   of friends was dead.

1310   Quickly Beowulf was called for;   the victorious warrior
Was fetched to the hall.   Before daybreak he came,
This noble leader,   with a number of his warriors,
To where the wise one   sat and wondered
Whether the Lord   would ever
Give him relief   from this recurring woe.
The renowned-in-battle   marched over the floor
With his companions   -- the hall-wood thundered --
Until he spoke words   to the King of the Danes,
The wise ruler,   and asked if he had,

1320   As was his desire,   passed an agreeable night.
               Hrothgar spoke   protector of the Scyldings:
"Ask not about joy!   Sorrow is alive again
For the Danish people.   Aeschere is dead,
The older brother   of Yrmenlaf;
He was my trusted counselor   and my advisor,
My shoulder companion   when in battle
We guarded our heads   as troops clashed together
And slashed at boar-emblems;   a good and noble man,
This Aeschere was   -- so should a warrior be!

1330   A wandering murderous spirit   slew him with her hands
Here in Heorot;   I know not whither
She dragged that proud corpse,   where she returned
To enjoy her feasting.   She has avenged the battle
Of last night   when you slew Grendel
With your hardy fists   in so compelling a fashion,
Because for so long   he had destroyed and diminished
My hall-thanes.   In that battle he fell,
His life was forfeit;   and now the other has come,
Mighty man-enemy,   to avenge her kin.

1340   And far has she pushed   in redressing that battle.

So must it seem   to many proud warriors
Who weep in their minds   for the treasure giver;
So deep a distress,   now that the hand lies dead
Which in every way   treated all so well.

         I have heard it said   by my people,
Both country-folk   and counselor,
That they have seen   two great
Wasteland-roamers   lurking on the moors,
  -- alien spirits.   The one was,
1350   So far as they   could tell with certainty,
In the likeness of a woman;   the other, wretched,
Trod in the form of a man   on the path of exile,
Except that he was larger   than any man;
In those long gone days   the people of this land
Called him Grendel;   they spoke of no father --
Whether before   they were begotten
By terrible dark things.   They roam the wolf slopes,
The windy headlands,   fearful fen paths,
The unfathomable places,   where the mountain stream,
1360   Under dark fogs,   tears its way downward
To the floods under ground.   It is not far from here
When measured in miles   that the lake lies;
Groves hang over it   covered with hoarfrost;
Woods with gnarled roots   bend into the water.
There each night   a strange marvel may be seen,
A glow in the water.   Of the children of men
None lives so wise   that he might understand that place.
Even the heath-stepper,   mighty strong-horned deer,
Harassed by hounds   and chased from afar,
1370   Will give up its life   in its race to safety,
Freely at the mere-edge,   before he will plunge in

To protect his head.   That place is not good.

And surging water   swirls up from there,

Dark to the clouds,   when the wind compels

Hostile storms,   until the air becomes gloomy

And the heavens weep.   Now again is help dependent

On you alone.   The region you know not,

That fearful place,   where you will find

That sin-filled thing;   seek her if you dare!

1380   I will pay you with riches   for that battle,

With ancient treasures   and twisted gold,

As I did before,   if you accept the charge!"

        Beowulf spoke,   Ecgtheow's son:

"Sorrow not, wise friend!   It is better for any

That he avenge his friend   than he mourn overmuch.

Each man who lives   must abide the end

Of life in this world;   who might may acquire

Glory before death;   that is afterwards best

For the warrior   whose days are at an end.

1390   Arise, ruler of the realm,   let us go quickly

To examine the track   of the kinswoman of Grendel.

I vow this to you: she will not make escape --

Neither in the bowels of earth   nor in the mountain wood,

Nor yet at the ocean bottom,   go where she will!

Have patience   this day

In spite of your woes,   as I expect you will."

The ancient one leapt up   and thanked God,

The Almighty Lord,   for what the man had spoken.

        Then was Hrothgar's   horse bridled,

1400   The curly-maned steed.   The wise old king

Rode along as befitted,   his band of shield-bearers

Following after.   The tracks were

Clearly seen   over the forest pathways,

Footprints along the ground,   as straight she went

Over the murky moor,   and carried along the best

Of the best of thanes,   lifeless,

He who with Hrothgar   had kept watch over the building.

The children of men   then went over

Towering rock-falls   and narrow pathways,

1410   Past cheerless cliffs,   lonely unknown valleys,

Precipitous bluffs   alive with water-monster lairs.

He with his best   rode out in front,

The wise warrior,   exploring the landscape,

Until he suddenly   came to mountain trees

Leaning close into   hoary boulders.

No joy in that forest.   The water below

Was blooded and murky.   And to all the Danes there

Was anxiety untold,   to all Scylding retainers,

Grief too great to endure;   to the warrior company,

1420   Distress down to the man,   when they came

Upon the head of Aeschere   lying on a high mere-cliff.

The men looked upon   lake water boiling with blood

And hot with gore.   The horn rang out and rang again

With a ready war song.   All the foot-troops sat.

At the mere-edge then they saw   many of serpent-kind,

Strange sea-dragons   sounding the water;

Water-things squirmed   low at the lake shore,

Like those in the mornings,   that most perilous of times,

That often make hazardous   the well known sea-ways --

1430   Wild creatures, worm-like.   They rushed away in rage,

Furious and frantic;   they had heard the clear sound,

The call of that battle horn.   A Geatish warrior

With the skill of his bow   put an end to the life

Of one sea-thrasher;   into its soft belly
Slammed a hard war-arrow;   it was the less
In swimming the waters   when the warrior killed it.
Still writhing in death throes,   it was stabbed with boar-spears,
Hard hooks of steel   that tore at its body,
Dragged to the hill-top   in spite of its bulk,
1440 This strange wave-roamer.   Men looked in silence
At this awesome water-terror.

                                          Beowulf made himself ready.
In his splendid war-gear   he feared not at all for his life.
His war-byrnie,   ample and finely wrought,
Woven by hand,   soon to be tested in the deep,
Was a fit thing   to protect his body,
So that the hostile grasp,   the malicious clutch,
Might not harm his heart   or take his life.
And his shining helmet,   adorned with jewels,
Circled all around with ornaments,   kept his head safe;
1450 It soon was to   visit the surging waters,
And to stir up the mere bottom;   in days of old it was
Made by the weapon-smith,   who formed it with wonders,
Set swine-likenesses on it,   so that ever after
Neither sword nor strong battle-ax   might cleave it.
And not the least   aid to his strength
Was the long-hilted sword,   Hrunting it was called,
That in his need   Hrothgar's spokesman offered;
It was the foremost   of the ancient treasures;
Bitter sharp the edge,   acid-carved the design,
1460 Tempered in war-blood;   never in battle did it forsake
Any strong warrior   who held it well,
Who dared to go   on a perilous journey
To the dreadful battle-ground;   nor was this the first time

That it had to perform   such valorous work.

Indeed, Ecglaf's kin,   who had great power,

Himself was without memory   of what he had said,

Drunk before with wine,   when he lent that weapon

To that better sword-warrior;   he himself dared not

Venture his life   under the turmoil of the waves

1470   To perform brave deeds;   lost was the chance of judgment

For valorous action.   It was not so with the other,

Once he had put on   his good battle gear.

        Beowulf spoke,   the son of Ecgtheow:

"Think now, glorious   son of Healfdene,

King full of wisdom,   gold-friend to men,

Now that I am eager to take   the journey we spoke of before,

If I at your bidding   should lose my life,

That you ever are to me   at my death

In a father's place,   and so you ever were.

1480   Be a guardian   of my young thanes,

My companions,   if battle takes me;

Also the treasures   which you have given me,

Precious Hrothgar,   send them on to Hygelac.

Perhaps in perceiving the gold,   the Geatish lord,

The son of Hrethel,   will see in the treasures

That I found a   willing ring-giver

High in generosity,   and that I enjoyed all while I could.

And let Unferth,   a famed man of men,

Have my ancient heirloom,   hard, wave-scrolled,

1490   Splendid sword.   I with Hrunting

Will seek my glory,   or death will take me!"

        After these words   the man of the Geats

Hastened with valor;   he did not need to wait

For an answer.   The surging water swallowed up

The battle-warrior.   Then a good part of the day passed
Before he could see   the bottom of the mere.
Almost at once   she who guarded those murky regions,
Grim and greedy,   fierce and ravenous,
And had for a hundred years,   was aware that some man
1500   Had come down from above   into the alien creature's region.
She grasped him then,   seized the battle-warrior
In her horrid hand-grip,   but none the sooner injured
His muscled flesh;   it was firmly protected in locked rings,
Hard war-dress, so that she   could not penetrate it,
Chest coat of mail,   with her hostile claws.
The sea-wolf then,   when she came to the bottom,
Bore the ringed prince   straight to her lair,
So that he could not   -- though he had the mind --
Wield his good weapons,   but many water-wonders
1510   Clawed and harassed him,   many sea-beasts
Slammed great tusks   into his battle-coat,
And persecuted the warrior.   Then the man perceived
That he was in the horrible lair   of his hostile host,
Where the water no longer   could do him harm,
Nor, because of the roofed-hall   might it touch him,
The flood's sudden attack.   He saw firelight,
Brilliant glitter,   bright flames.

The good one then beheld   the accursed monster,
The mighty mere-woman;   he gave a huge thrust
1520   With his battle-sword;   he did not hold back,
So that on her head   the ring-marked sword sang
Its greedy war-song.   Then the guest there found
That the flashing sword   was of no use,
Could do her no harm.   The sword had failed
The prince in his need;   before it had endured many

Hard meetings,   had often cut through helmets
And doomed war garments;   that was the first time
For the precious treasure   that its glory was less.

       Again he was resolute,   the kinsman of Hygelac;
1530   He was mindful of fame,   committed to glory:
He cast away the curve-etched sword   bound with ornaments,
Hardened and steel-edged,   so that it lay on the ground.
A warrior enraged,   he trusted his strength
And the might of his hand-grip.   So must a man do
When he at the battle   thinks to gain
Long lasting praise;   he must care not for his life.
The man of the Geats   seized then by the shoulder
The mother of Grendel   -- not at all shrunk from that fight --
In fury fierce,   at the battle enraged.
1540   He flung the deadly foe   so that she fell to the floor.
She paid him in kind   quickly for that fall;
With grim-grasp   she clashed against him.
The weary-in-spirit,   the best of the best of men,
Splendid foot-warrior,   weakened, fell over.
Then she sat upon this hall-visitor,   drew out her knife,
Broad and age-colored;   she wished to avenge her son,
The only kinsman she had.   Covering him to his shoulder lay
The light-ringed byrnie;   it protected his life
Against spear point, sword edge,   kept his chest safe.
1550   The son of Ecgtheow,   the Geatish warrior,
Would have then perished   under the dirt-roof
If his war-corselet had not   given him help,
That hard battle-net   -- and the Holy God
Brought about war-victory;   the wise Lord,
The Ruler of Heaven,   decided on right,
Easily,   when he got to his feet.

He spied then in the battle   a victorious sword,
An old sword with a strong edge,   made by giants
As an honor to men;   that was the best of weapons,

1560   Except that it was greater   than any other man
Might have borne   into battle;
Good it was and splendid,   the handiwork of giants.
He seized the linked-hilt,   the friend of the Scyldings,
Savage and sword-grim,   drew the ring-marked sword,
Despairing of life,   and angrily struck
So that against her neck   the weapon slammed hard;
Her spine broke;   the sword went full through
Her doomed body;   she fell to the floor dead.
The sword was bloody;   the man rejoiced in his work.

1570   Gleaming flashed out,   a light from the cave glittered,
Even as heaven's candle   lights up the sky,
Glorious in radiance.   He gazed along the building,
Then turned to the wall,   raised up the weapon
Hard by the hilt,   Hygelac's thane,
Angry and resolute.   Its edge was not useless
To the battle-warrior,   and he quickly chose
To repay Grendel   for the many attacks
He had successfully made   on the Danish people,
Much more often   than that one time

1580   When Hrothgar's   hearth-companions
He slew while they slumbered,   lying asleep --
Fifteen men,   Scylding warriors;
And another such group   he carried back to his lair,
Loathly and hostile.   He paid him for that,
This fierce warrior,   battle weary,
For there he   saw Grendel lying
Lifeless,   as he was destroyed

In the battle at Heorot.   The corpse burst open
When long after death   it suffered a gash,
1590   A hard battle-stroke,   as he cut off his head.

Soon then they saw   -- the wise men
Who gazed at the water   while waiting with Hrothgar --
That the surging waves   grew stained with crimson,
Were oozing with blood.   The gray-haired men,
The ancient ones,   spoke together about the good warrior,
And they did not think   that he,
Victorious,   would ever see again
The great ruler;   then many decided
That the water-wolf   had cut him down.
1600   It was the ninth hour of the day.   The valiant Scyldings
Gave up the cliffs;   the gold-friend of men
Turned himself towards home,   and the strangers sat,
Sick in spirit,   staring at the mere;
They wished but did not expect   to ever see again
Their friendly-lord himself.   Then that sword,
That war-weapon,   after the blood-fight
Began to waste away   in battle-icicles;
It was a marvelous wonder   when it began to melt,
Most like the ice   when the Father unleashes the frost,
1610   Uncurls it like a rope;   He who has control
Of seasons of all and times of all,   He truly is God.
He took nothing from that place,   the man of the Geats,
Took none of the treasures,   although he saw many there --
Only the great head   and the bejeweled hilt
Together: the sword had already melted;
The blade had burned.   The venomous blood of the alien spirit
Who had died in the hall   was too hot by far!
Soon he was swimming,   he who before at battle had survived

The war-fall of hostile foes,   moving up through the water.

1620 The tossing waves suddenly   were everywhere clean,

Purged altogether,   when the alien creature

Gave up the passing of days   and the sorrows of life.

The protector of sea-men   then reached the shore,

Swimming stout-heartedly;   he rejoiced in the sea-booty,

In the mighty burden   he had brought with him.

The splendid company of thanes   thanked the Good Lord

And went then to meet him;   they rejoiced in the prince

Now that they could see   him safe on the shore.

Then from the vigorous one   were the helmet and byrnie

1630 Happily removed.   The lake was quiet,

The water stained slaughter-red   under the clouds.

They went forth then   along the known footpaths;

Rejoicing in their hearts   they moved along speedily,

At peace with the way.   The king-brave troop

Took up the head   from the mere cliff --

No easy task;   each one of them helped

In their bravery;   two pairs of two

Lugged the battle-pike   and Grendel's head

To the gold-hall,   and still it was difficult.

1640 Presently then   they came close to the hall.

Bold and warlike,   the band of fourteen

Geat warriors,   their courageous lord in the troop

With them,   trod the plains near the mead-hall.

And then the chief   of these war-thanes,

The man daring in deeds,   adorned with glory,

The warrior brave in battle,   went in to greet Hrothgar.

Then Grendel's head   was carried by the hair

Into the hall   where the men were drinking;

It was a terror for the men   and the women with them,

1650   A wondrous spectacle;   they looked in awe!

                Beowulf spoke,   the son of Ecgtheow:

"True, this sea-booty,   son of Healfdene,

Prince of the Scyldings,   we have brought happily to you

As a token of glory.   See it before you now!

I willingly endured   that unsoft task,

That war under water,   dared the work

That was not easy;   the battle would have been short,

Over at once,   had not God protected me.

Nor at the battle   could I accomplish a thing

1660   With Hrunting,   for all of its power;

But the Lord of all men   -- He who is most often

The guide of the friendless --   granted to me

That I saw on the wall   a sword hanging,

Large and old and beautiful,   and I drew that weapon.

I slew then at the battle,   when I saw my chance,

The keeper of that hall.   Then the battle-sword,

Wave-etched the blade,   melted as the blood bolted out,

So hot was that battle-sweat.   I carried the hilt

Away from the fiend   and avenged the hostile deeds,

1670   The deathly Danish slaughter,   as I should have done.

I promise to you now   that you might sleep without sorrow

In Heorot,   you with your troop of men,

And each thane   of your people,

Ancient or youthful,   you need not fear for them,

Prince of the Scyldings,   fear not for their deaths,

From the source   you before had to endure."

Then the golden hilt   was placed in the hands

Of the aged warrior,   given to the grizzled battle-chief,

The work of wonder-smiths,   fashioned by giants so long before.

1680   After the fall of devils   it passed into the hands

Of the Danish king,   and when the hostile-hearted man,

Guilty of murder and more,   the enemy of God,

And his mother, too,   gave up this world,

It came into the control   of the earthly king,

The best there was   between the two seas,

The greatest giver of treasures   to the Danish people.

Hrothgar spoke,   first examining the hilt,

The ancient treasure.   On it was written

Of the ancient strife,   when the flood,

1690   The rush of the ocean,   slew the race of giants,

Who knew terrible woes;   that was a people estranged

To the eternal God.   The Ruler imposed

The surge of the flood   for their final requital.

And on the hilt   -- glorious, gold-worked,

Engraved in decoration   in ordered runes --

Was the name of the man   for whom the sword,

That best of weapons,   twisted hilt, snake embossed,

First was worked.   Then the wise one spoke,

The son of Healfdene,   and all were silent:

1700   "Now may he say,   who in truth and might

Acts for the people   and remembers the past

And the old kings of our land,   that this man was

Born the better!   Your glory is raised up

Around all of earth's realms,   my friend Beowulf,

Your fame to all people.   You hold steady

Your great might with a wise spirit.   I shall keep you friend

As we spoke of before.   You shall prove a source of consolation

To your people,   to all be granted for years to come

A warrior to help.

Heremod was not so

1710   To the offspring of Ecgwela,   the Scylding warriors;

He grew, not to joy   but to great slaughter
And to destruction   of the Danish people;
Inflamed, he cut down   his table companions
And his battle-companions,   until alone, he turned away,
Famous ruler of the people,   from the joys of life among men,
Although mighty God   had exalted him
In strength and in pleasure,   had advanced him further
Than all other men.   However, his spirit began to beat
Bloodthirsty in his breast;   he gave nothing of value
1720   To the Danes in glory;   joyless he lived
Until he suffered   for the great struggle,
His people's enduring affliction.   Take this from that:
Act like a man!   I make this speech to you
From the depths of my years.

                       What wonder in the telling --
How mighty God   through His own generosity
Gives wisdom   to mankind,
And land and position;   He controls all things.
Sometimes out of love   He permits delighting
Of thought to a man   of the highest order,
1730   Gives such a man   all worldly pleasures,
Good shelter for his followers   to his holding;
Great realms,   vast regions
Seem his to control,   such that he cannot
In his foolishness   think that it will ever end.
He remains at feasting;   sickness and old age
Come not to him,   not to him sorrow;
He knows no dark spirit,   nor is enmity anywhere
In sword-hate manifest;   but all the world
Goes as he wishes.   He knows no worse,
1740   Until in his spirit   an abundance of pride

Grows and then flourishes   when the keeper sleeps,

The watchman of his soul;   that sleep too complete!

Then bound by his affliction,   and the killer at hand

Who from his bow   shoots shafts so evil,

In spite of his armor   then is his heart hit

With a bitter arrow   -- guard himself he cannot.

But by perverse suggestions   from the evil one

He thinks too little   what he held too long,

And he covets in anger,   never thinks to dispense

1750   Golden treasures,   and he his destiny

Forgets, unremembering   what God the Dispenser of Wonders

Had given to him before,   in honor and great plenty.

In the end, as always,   it comes to pass

That the body   weakens and declines,

And doomed, it falls;   yet another seizes control,

And recklessly   gives out treasures,

Ancient heirlooms of men,   nor heeds any fear.

Guard yourself from that evil,   beloved Beowulf,

Best of men,   and choose what is better.

1760   Provide for the eternal;   heed not pride,

Great champion!   Now is your might for a time

In glory;   soon now it will be that

Sickness or sword,   or flight of the spear,

Horrid old age,   or the eye's brightness

Fails and becomes dim;   presently it is,

Good-warrior,   that death will overpower you.

So did I rule the Danes   for fifty winters,

1770   Held them under the skies,   protected them from warfare,

From many of the tribes   from around this earth,

Against spear and sword,   well enough that I feared

No people who lived   anywhere under the heavens.

True it is, that to me in my own country   reversal was to befall,
Grief after gladness,   when Grendel came,
My old adversary,   my invader;
I bore the persecution   continually, without end,
Great anguish of mind.   Then be God thanked,
The eternal Lord,   that I abided long enough
1780 To see on that head   blood from the battle-sword,
End to the struggle.   I see it so joyously!
Go now to the seat,   take part in the feast,
Distinguished in battle;   With you I shall share
A large number of treasures   when morning comes."
         The Geat was glad at heart,   immediately went there
And sought out a seat   as the wise one ordered.
Then it was as it had been   for the courageous ones
Sitting in the hall.   A bounteous feast had been prepared
Again, once more.   The cover of night fell
1790 Dark over the retainers.   The warriors all stood;
The gray-haired one wished   to go to his bed,
The ancient Scylding.   The Geat in glory resplendent,
Renowned shield-warrior,   was weary for his rest,
Exhausted from the going   in the far country;
At once the chamberlain   showed him the way,
He who in courtesy   attended to all
The needs of each thane,   much as in those ancient days
Good sea-warriors   might have had done.
The noble-spirited one then rested.   The hall stood high,
1800 Vaulted and gold-adorned;   the guest within slept
Until the black raven   cheerfully announced
The joy of heaven.   Then the light came,
Dappling the shadows;   the warriors hastened.
The retainers were   eager to begin to go

Back to their people;   the one bold of spirit
Himself was anxious to inspect his ship   and to be away.

The brave one then called   for Hrunting to be brought
To the son of Ecglaf;   said to take back the sword,
That lovely iron,   said thanks for the gift,
1810   Said he considered   that war-friend good,
Strong in battle,   could by no means find fault
With the edge of that blade.   There was a gallant man!
And then eager to depart,   with war-gear at hand,
The warriors were ready;   the one valued by the Danes,
The man brave-in-battle,   went to the raised seat
Where the old one was,   and greeted Hrothgar.

Beowulf spoke,   the son of Ecgtheow:
"Now is the time for we seafarers   having come so far,
To say that we   are eager to go
1820   To seek Hygelac.   We were here with all of our desires
Most properly attended to;   you have done us well.
If I here on earth   may do anything further
To earn your love   the more deeply,
Lord of warriors,   than I have already done
In battle-deeds,   I will be ready at once.
If it comes to me   over the vast oceans
That you are threatened with terror   by neighboring tribes,
As they so often   have done before,
I will bring to you   a thousand thanes,
1830   Soldiers to your aid.   I know that Hygelac,
My Geatish leader,   shepherd of his people,
Although he be young,   will support me
With words and works,   so that I may further
Honor and help you,   bring spear shafts to you,
And thus support you,   where to you is need of men.

If then Hrethric,   your chief son,

Thinks of the Geatish court,   he will find there

Many a true friend;   the far country is better sought

By the man   who has bettered himself."

1840   Hrothgar spoke   and made answer to him:

"These words the wise Ruler of all   has sent

To your heart;   I have never heard

A man so young   speak words so true.

You are resolute in strength   and wise in spirit,

Mature in your speech!   I know full well

If it happens   that war should take

The son of Hrethel,   your elder

And guardian of your people,   by bloody battle-sword --

Sword, say, or sickness --   and you have life,

1850   That the sea-Geats   could never make

Better choice of king,   guardian of the treasures of men,

Than yourself would be   if you should agree to

Rule in your land.   Your true worth

Grows as my knowledge of you grows,   beloved Beowulf.

You have brought it about   that our nations,

The Geatish people   and the Danish people,

Have concurred in peace,   and have stopped the fighting

And the hostility   which they before suffered;

And, so long as   I control the wide lands,

1860   Treasures will be shared,   and many a one

Will give gifts to another   over the gannet's bath;

Ring-prowed ships will   bring over the sea

Gifts and tokens of love.   I know our people

Against enemies and friends   are now fastened in firmness,

In every respect blameless,   as it was so long ago."

        Then in that high hall   the son of Healfdene,

The protector of warriors,   gave him twelve treasures.

Said he should go with the gifts   to his own dear people,

To seek them in safety,   speedily return again.

1870   The good king   of the Scylding people

Then kissed the best warrior,   grasping him

By the neck;   his gray beard held

The tears he could not keep back.   Old and wise,

He knew two things,   but one most especially,

That they never again   would see one another,

The courageous in council.   The man was so dear to him

That he felt an ache in his heart   great beyond enduring.

And in that heart,   bound with strings of love,

A hidden longing   for the dear man

1880   Burned in his blood.   From him Beowulf,

The gold-adorned battle-warrior,   trod towards the shore,

Rejoicing in the treasures.   The great ship

Awaited its lord,   straining at anchor.

As they walked   the gifts of Hrothgar

Were often praised;   he was one king

Altogether faultless   -- until old age

Took the delights of his strength,   as it so often does.

       The very brave ones then   came to the sea,

Young warrior company;   they wore ringed byrnies,

1890   Linked coats of mail.   The guard of the coast perceived

The men on their return journey,   as he had before;

From the top of the cliffs   and not with an insult

Did he greet the visitors,   but he rode towards them,

Then gave welcome   to the Weder-warriors,

Soldiers in bright armor   on their way to the ship.

Then on the sand   was the spacious ship

Loaded with battle-armor,   the ring-prowed ship,

With horses and treasures;   the mast towered
Over Hrothgar's   precious gifts.
1900   He gave then   to the boat-guard
A sword of twisted gold,   so that later
At the mead-bench   he was the more valued
For that precious heirloom.   The ship then set out,
Churned a wide wake,   left the land of the Danes.
Then on the mast   a great sail was set,
Was fastened with tackle;   the sea-wood groaned,
Nor did the waves   hinder the journey.
The ship,   the great sea-goer,
Foamy-necked,   slipped forth over the waves;
1910   The craft with bound prow   sailed over the water-streams
Until they could perceive   the Geatish cliffs,
The bluffs familiar to them.   The vessel pressed forward,
Driven by wind,   and beached at the shore.
Quickly the guard of the harbor   was at the ship,
He who for a long time before,   longing for the sea,
Had searched   for the beloved warriors;
He fastened the roomy ship   there on the sand,
Anchored it firmly,   lest the force of the waves
Might drive the winsome wood   loose to the sea.
1920   He then ordered them to carry up   the great treasures,
Precious and gold-plated things;   it was not far from there
For him to find   the treasure-giver,
Hygelac Hrethling,   and where he dwelt at home,
Himself with his retainers,   there by the sea-wall.
        The building was splendid,   high the hall
Of that valiant king,   and Hygd very young,
But accomplished in wisdom   and courtly delights
Under the castle enclosure,   though the winters were few

To that daughter of Haereth.   Nor was she illiberal,

1930   Niggardly in gifts   to the Geatish people,

Neither in treasures.   Thryth, however,

Renowned queen of the people,   performed terrible crimes.

None there was,   among even her own retainers,

Who dared the boldness   to glance at her

Even in broad daylight,   except that greatest of lords,

But any other could count   on the deadly bonds

Of hand-woven rope,   a seizing of hands,

And quickly thereupon   the wave-etched sword,

Harsh mediation   to settle everything --

1940   Evil bringer of death.   Such deeds are not queenly,

Nor acts of a woman,   however beautiful,

When a gentle peace-weaver,   pretending injury,

Deprives men in her service   of their life and breath.

The kinsman of Hemming   stopped that at once:

Warriors at ale drinking   would finish the tale,

Say she was guilty of   far fewer outrages,

Hostile acts to the people,   when she was given,

Gold adorned and radiant   to that young warrior

Of the highest cut,   after she had come

1950   At her father's bidding   over the great ocean

To the hall of Offa.   There she lived after,

Her throne glorious   for the gifts she gave.

She made best use   of the days of her life,

Held high-love   for the chief of the warriors,

Known to all of men   in the highest renown,

The best of the best   in all of the world

Between the two seas.   Therefore Offa was

For gifts as for battle   so widely honored,

The spear-brave warrior;   in wisdom he held

1960   His native land;   then from him Eomer woke,
           A help to the warriors,   kinsman to Hemming
           Grandson to Garmund,   skillful in battle.
               The hard one then went   with his companions,
           Walked along the shore,   close by the water,
           Vast stretch by the sea.   The sky-candle shone,
           The jewel hastening from the south.   They made the journey,
           Going valiantly   to where they knew
           The young warrior-protector,   the slayer of Ongentheow
           And good battle-king,   distributed rings
1970   Within the castle.   Hygelac was
           Quickly told   of the coming of Beowulf
           To his enclosure;   the protector of warriors,
           Of shield-companions,   had come, alive,
           Back from the battle-play   and was returning to court.
           Quickly it was made ready,   as the mighty one ordered;
           The floor within was cleared   for the foot-warriors.
               He sat then with him,   he who survived the battle,
           Kinsman with kinsman,   after he had greeted
           His lord as a friend,   with forceful words
1980   In a formal court speech.   The daughter of Haereth,
           Who loved the people,   bore cups of strong drink
           Around that hall-building,   gave cups of clear mead
           To the hands of the warriors.   Hygelac began then
           To courteously question   his companion at table
           In that highest of halls;   curiosity broke over him,
           How the Geat   journey had gone:
           "How did it befall to you,   beloved Beowulf,
           When you suddenly   resolved to journey,
           Seek in battle   far over the salty water
1990   Valor in Heorot?   Ah, did you Hrothgar's

Widely-known woe   a whit find the remedy

For that great prince?   I brooded over the soul-sorrow

Of surging cares;   I had no faith in the journey,

Beloved man of men;   I ever asked that you

Greet not at all   the murderous spirit,

But let the Danes   themselves make battle

Against Grendel.   To God I give thanks

That I once more   am able to see you safe."

       Beowulf spoke,   the son of Ecgtheow:

2000   "That great encounter,   lord Hygelac,

Is not kept hidden   from many men,

How battle-time fell   to Grendel and me

In that great hall   where he had brought sorrow

To so many   of the Scylding warriors,

And misery sufficient.   I avenged that in full,

So none of Grendel's kin   from all of the earth,

Not any of the hostile ones,   enveloped in malice,

Can find reason to boast   over who lived the longest

In that darkest part of night.   I first came

2010   To the ring-hall   to greet Hrothgar;

Soon the great   kinsman of Healfdene,

When he knew   my firm intentions,

Assigned me a seat   next to his own son.

The troop was in delight;   I have never seen far or wide

Under the wide arch of heaven   sitters in the hall

More joyous at mead.   Now and again the glorious queen,

Pledging peace to the people,   passed over all of that floor,

Urging on the young boys;   each time she gave

Rings to the men;   then she went to her seat.

2020   Sometimes to the warriors   the daughter of Hrothgar

Bore the ale-cup,   went to even the furthest;

I heard the men there   give her name

As Freawaru,   she who carried the studded cup,

And gave it to the warriors.   She is promised,

Young and gold-adorned,   to the mannerly son of Froda;

The friend of the Scyldings,   who holds the kingdom,

Has given his word,   and considers it good council --

He with the woman   the fateful feuding

And battles will settle.   But full seldom anywhere,

2030   After the fall of a prince,   except for a time,

Will the deadly-spear rest,   no matter the bride.

        The lord of the Heathobards   may then be displeased,

And each of his thanes,   those best of men,

When he with the maiden   moves through the hall;

When Danish nobility   and the warriors are attended to,

And on them glistening,   ancient heirlooms,

Hard and wave-etched,   Heathobard treasures --

Theirs so long as they were able   to wield those weapons,

        Until shield-play   led to their destruction

2040   Of their dear companions   and their own lives.

Then an old foot soldier   who gazes at the sword-hilt

At the drinking of beer,   remembering the whole story --

The spear-death of the warriors   -- his heart grows black --

And he begins in a mournful spirit   to tempt the mind

Of a young warrior,   baleful his heart-urgings,

To stir up war-thoughts.   He says these words:

'Do you not, my friend,   recognize the sword

That your father   bore into battle,

Brave in his war gear,   that one last time,

2050   Dearest of swords,   when the Danes killed him?

They held the battle-field   against the vigorous Scyldings,

Until Withergyld fell   and the warriors fell.

And now there a son   of one of the killers,

Exulting in his heirloom,   goes as he pleases about the floor,

Boasts of the murders,   and carries the treasure

Which should be yours   in all right council.'

He keeps at his chiding,   reproving with bitter words

At every occasion,   until the time comes

That the lady's thane,   for the death of his father,

2060   Sleeps blood-stained   after the bite of the sword,

Having forfeited his life.   And the slayer will flee,

Escape with his life,   for the land is familiar to him.

Then is shattered   on both sides

The oaths of warriors,   after Ingeld

Rages in deadly hate,   and in the seething of sorrows,

The love for his peace-weaver   becomes the cooler.

Thus I think little   of the Heathobard gesture,

Think that such alliance,   sincerity to the Danes,

Is far from fast friendship.

I shall now speak

2070   Further about Grendel   so that you may know clearly,

Giver of treasures,   what was the course

Of that monumental hand-match.   After the jewel of heaven

Had passed over the earth,   the hostile spirit,

The horrid demon enraged by the dark,   came to seek us out,

Where we unharmed   guarded the hall.

There Hondscio was   fated to die horribly;

In a deadly battle   that girdled warrior

Was the first to fall.   Grendel became to him,

To that good retainer,   a flesh-hungry killer;

2080   He completely devoured   the beloved man's body.

He made no haste;   the bloody tooth-slayer,

Mindful of destruction,   was in no hurry

To leave the gold-hall,   and not empty-handed.

But he wished to try me   with his renowned might,

Grasped me with ready-hand.   His glove hung,

Large and wonderful,   fast with cunning stitches.

It was everywhere   adorned with

Devil's markings,   fashioned of dragon skins.

The bold evil-doer   wanted to stuff me there,

2090   Unsinning,   one of many

Inside that pouch.   It was not to be so;

When I stood up,   my spirit inflamed.

Too long is the telling,   how I gave requital

To that man-enemy   for each of his evils;

There, my lord,   I honored your people

With my deeds.   He fled then,

Escaped for a little time   to relish life's joys,

But his stronger hand   remained behind,

His right hand in Heorot,   and mournful in spirit,

2100   In his wretchedness   he sank to the bottom of the mere.

For the bloody conflict   the Scylding king,

Paid me in full   with much ornamented gold

And splendid treasures,   when morning came

And we had set   to a banquet prepared.

Then were tales and entertainments;   the ancient Scylding,

Schooled in such things,   recounted the far past.

Sometimes the one brave in battle   brought joy from the harp,

That wood of mirth,   sometimes told a song

Of truth and sadness,   sometimes wove a strange spell

2110   Relating what is right,   this large-hearted king.

Now and again he began,   bound by old age,

The ancient battle-warrior,   to speak of his youth,

His battle strength;   wise in winters

His heart railed within him   when he remembered it all.

So in that great hall   all the day long

We took our pleasure   until night fell

Once more to men.   Then again quickly it was

That Grendel's mother   came sorrowfully,

Eager to avenge that injury.   Death had taken her son

2120   In the war with the Weders.   The monstrosity of woman

Avenged her son,   killed a warrior

In a bold fashion;   that one, taken from life,

Was Aeschere,   a wise old counselor.

Nor could they,   the Danish people,

When morning came   burn the dead man,

Set flames to a pyre   that held his beloved body,

Taken by death;   she lugged off the carcass

In an unholy embrace,   fled down under the mountain stream.

To Hrothgar that was   the most bitter of the distresses

2130   That leader of the people   had suffered so long.

Then the troubled prince   implored me

By your life,   that I in baleful waters

Should venture my spirit,   should do heroic deeds,

Should attend to glory.   He promised me reward.

It is well known   that in those surging waters

I found the grim and terrible   guardian of the deep.

For a long while there   it was hand against hand;

The water boiled with blood;   and in that battle

I cut off the head   of the mother of Grendel

2140   With a mighty sword;   with difficulty I escaped

From that awful place;   I was not yet fated to die.

The protector of men,   Healfdene's son,

Again gave me   abundance of treasures.

And the king of the people   lived according to custom;

Nothing I did   would have lost me those treasures,

Rewards for my strength;   he offered me heirlooms,

Healfdene's son,   and it is my own wish,

King of warriors,   that I bring them to you,

Gifts with all my good will.   Further, all joy at hand

2150   Now depends on you;   I have few

Near relatives, Hygelac,   but for you."

He then ordered brought in   the boar-banner, the

great banner,

The steep battle helmet,   the gray-linked byrnie,

The splendid battle-sword,   and spoke this speech:

"Hrothgar gave to me   this war dress,

A most wise king;   he asked that first

I say to you   the history of this gear,

Said that king Heorogar   held it all first,

Man of the Scyldings,   and for a long while.

2160   No sooner for that   would he give to his son,

To the valiant Heoroweard,   though he loved him,

The chain-linked coat.   Enjoy it all fully."

It is said that   four matched horses,

Bays, were brought in quickly   after the treasures,

Followed hard upon;   he granted them both,

Riches and treasures.   So should a kinsman do,

Never a net of malice   weave for others --

Evil that craft -- ,   nor devise the death

Of a close companion.   In that hard battle,

2170   The nephew of Hygelac   was exceedingly faithful,

And each to the other   was a source of joy.

It was said that then he gave   the golden collar to Hygd,

The wondrous treasure   that Wealhtheow gave to him,

Daughter of a prince,   together with three horses,

Supple, shining-saddled;   after the gold-giving,
The brilliant necklace   adorned her breast.

The son of Ecgtheow   had thus shown his bravery,
Was renowned in battles,   famous for good deeds,
Held himself for judgment;   his companions in drinking
2180 Were safe in his hands;   nor was his heart savage,
But the brave in battle   kept safe
The greatest of gifts,   the largesse of God,
The greatest might of all mankind.   As a youth he was humiliated,
Long the Geatish warriors   reckoned no good in him,
Nor did the lord of the Weders   think to grant
Many treasures at all   to him at the mead-bench.
It was generally thought   that he was lazy,
Was slow to action.   But reversal was to come
To the glorious warrior   for each of those thoughts.
2190 The protector of men,   the battle-brave king,
Ordered Hrethel's sword   to be brought in,
The gold-worked treasure;   there was not among the Geats
A better heirloom   in the form of a sword;
He put it into   Beowulf's lap,
And gave him   seven thousand --
In a great hall and lands.   To the both of them
In that country   was inherited lands,
Ancestral regions,   and to the more illustrious
Greater riches,   as befitted his rank.
(EXTRA SPACE)
2200   It happened then,   after the passing of time,
In the crash of battle,   when Hygelac lay dead,
And Heardred,   under cover of shield
Was put to death   by battle-swords
Where they sought him out   among the victorious people,

The Heatho-Scyldings,   fierce warriors --
Attacked him by force,   this nephew of Hereric.
In this time then   the vast kingdom
Passed into the hands of Beowulf.   He ruled properly
For fifty winters   -- there was a wise king,
2210   An old guardian of the land -- ,   until a certain one,
A dragon began to rule   in the dark nights.
On the high heath   it guarded over a treasure
In a steep stone barrow;   a path lay beneath it
Unknown to men.   Close by there moved
Some man or other   who passed in near
The heathen hoard;   he seized a jeweled flagon
In his hand;   the dragon after that avenged it,
However he in sleeping   was tricked
By a thief's craft.   The people learned,
2220   All the neighboring folk,   that he was enraged.

                 Not at all of his own accord,   of his own will,
Did he break into the dragon's hoard   and do him injury,
But for sad necessity,   as someone's servant,
Some man among men,   he fled hostile blows,
And lacking a home,   penetrated within,
A man with the affliction of sin.   Immediately . . . .
That . . . . . the visitor   (. . . . terror) horror arose;
Yet the wretched   . . . .
2230   . . . .   horror overwhelmed him.
The precious flagon . . . . .

                          Many such riches
Lay in that barrow,   ancient treasures
From days so long before,   when some man
In his deep thoughts   had hidden them there,
That immense legacy,   the precious treasures

- 73 -

Of the princely kind.   Death took them all
From those ancient days,   yet one man remained
From the body of that people;   he moved there alone,
A guardian mourning his friends,   knowing well his fate.

2240   He had but little time   that he might
Enjoy those treasures.   The mound was quite ready,
Remained in that place   near the watery waves,
Newly made by the bluffs,   the entrance well hidden.
There within   the guardian of rings
Lugged down the treasure,   a hoard-worthy pile,
Rich ornamented gold,   and said these few words:
"Hold you now, earth,   now that heroes cannot,
These riches of men --   even as good men took it from you
In days now long past.   That horrible deadly evil,

2250   Battle death,   has taken each man
Of my people;   they have given up this life,
Seen the last of hall-joys.   I know of none who might carry the
                                                      sword,
Or might cleanse   the gold-plated cup,
That dear drinking vessel.   That noble band has departed.
The hard helmet,   adorned with gold,
Must be deprived of gold plate;   the polisher sleeps
Who should prepare   that war-mask;
And so the coat of mail   which endured iron bites
Above the crashing shields   at battle,

2260   Decays as the warrior.   Nor may the ringed-byrnie
Travel far after   the war-chief,
At the side of the hero.   Now no joy of harp,
No glee-wood joy.   Now no good hawk
Slashing through the hall.   Now no swift horse
Bursting through the castle court.   Baleful death

Has taken many   of the race of men."
So, sad of heart,   he uttered the sorrow
Of one after all,   and unhappily wandered about,
Both day and night,   until death's surging
2270   Harassed his heart.   An old night-enemy
Found the joy-hoard   standing open;
Enveloped in flames,   he flies at night,
Searching out such mounds,   is his best at burning,
This bare hostile dragon.   He is no friend
To the people of earth.   It is his lot
To seek the hoard in the earth,   where he heathen gold
Will guard for years beyond telling;   he is no better for that!
        For three hundred years   this scavenger scourge,
Awesome in power,   held that treasure house
2280   Deep in the earth,   until one man
Aroused his wrath;   this one bore off
The golden cup   as a compact of peace
To his lord for his sins.   The treasure was explored,
The ring-hoard lessened,   the favor granted
To the wretched man.   His lord examined
That ancient handiwork   for the first time.
When the dragon awoke   strife was awakened;
Writhing eagerly over the stones,   the terror found
The enemy foot-tracks,   where he in silence,
2290   In his secret craft,   had stepped near to the dragon's head.
So may an unfated man   easily endure peril,
And woe and exile,   when he stays
In the grace of the Ruler!   The hoard-ruler searched
Anxiously over the ground,   eager to find the man
Who handed sorrow to him   while he slept.
Hot with anger, fierce,   he flailed his way

Around and around the barrow --   and not a man
Lingered in that waste --   the dragon rejoiced in his rage,
In works of war;   returned at times to the barrow
2300   To seek the precious cup;   and he realized at last
That one of mankind   had tampered with his gold,
With his splendid treasures.   The hoard-guard waited,
Impatient for the dark,   until evening came.
The guard of the cave   rejoiced in his rage.
That ferocious one   would repay his foe with fire
For the loss of his precious cup.   When the day passed
The dragon was in joy;   no longer by the wall
Was he forced to wait,   but he went, enveloped in evil,
Infused with fire.   That beginning was terrible
2310   To the people of the land,   and quickly it became
A sore evil   for the ring-giver as well.

Then the visitor   began to spew out fire,
To burn the happy dwellings   -- the glow of the flames brought

forth

Horror to men.   Not one alive there
Would the hostile   air-flyer permit.
The dragon's destruction   was seen everywhere,
Near and far --   his cruelly hostile affliction -- ,
How that enemy   persecuted and humbled
The Geatish people,   and then hastened again to the hoard,
2320   To his hidden great-hall,   before the day came.
He had encircled in flames   the people of the land,
In flames and in fire;   and he trusted the barrow, its walls,
And his war-fire;   but his trust had deceived him.

Then to Beowulf   the terror was made clear,
The truth came to him   because of his own hall,
That best of buildings,   was burnt in a raging fire,

Gift-throne of the Geats.   Then the good man felt

A deep ache in his breast,   a great heart-sorrow,

For in his wisdom he believed   that he had sorely offended

2330   The great Ruler,   the eternal Lord,

Because of some ancient law;   deep within his breast

Such dark thoughts lurked   as were unknown to him.

The fire dragon had   consumed with flames

The stronghold of the people   on the land along the shore;

The fortress was ravaged.   For that the battle-king

Of the Weder people   devised his revenge.

The protector of warriors,   this ruler of men,

Ordered them to make for him   a wondrous battle-shield

Of nothing but iron;   he knew well

2340   That a wooden shield   would not help him,

Wood against fire.   The king from old times

Was to finish his life's days,   was to abide the end

Of his stay in this world,   together with dragon,

However long it had held   the treasure-hoard.

The ring-giving prince   scorned to approach

The far-flyer   with a company of men,

With a large host,   nor did he dread fighting him.

Not did he fear   the strength and the valor

Of the dragon,   because he before many

2350   Difficulties had dared,   hostilities had survived,

And battle flames,   when he had purged

Hrothgar's hall,   warrior graced with victory,

And at battle crushed   Grendel's kin

Of the hated kind.

Not the least was

The hand to hand clashing   where Hygelac was slain,

When the king of the Geats,   friendly lord of the people,

Hrethrel's son,   warring in the battle
In Friesland,   was bathed in battle-blood,
Beaten down by sword.   Then Beowulf came away,
2360 Swimming with all his might,   revealed his strength,
Had in his arms   on his own thirty
Battle-coats   when he went to the sea.
Not at all did the Hetware   find cause to exult
When they came forward   to fight on foot,
Moving shields against him;   few returned
From that warrior   to seek their homes!
The son of Ecgtheow,   forlorn and alone,
Swam over the sea regions   again to the people;
There Hygd offered him   the kingdom and riches,
2370 All its great treasures;   she did not believe
That her son was able   to hold the throne
Against a foreign people   now that Hygelac was dead.
No sooner for that   did the deprived
Folk find   that by any means
Would he be persuaded   to become lord over Heardred,
Or choose   to take the kingdom;
Nonetheless, he held him   high in good council,
And honor before the people,   until he was older
And could rule the Geats.

                              The outcasts came,
2380 Sought him out from over the sea,   the sons of Ohthere;
They had rebelled against   the lord of the Scylfings,
That best of the best   of all the sea-kings,
Who gave out riches   in Swedish lands,
Illustrious prince!   That marked the end
For Hygelac's son,   got him a mortal wound;
For his kind hospitality   was a harsh stroke of sword;

And the son of Ongentheow   turned away

To seek out his own home,   once Heardred lay dead,

Letting Beowulf hold   the seat of princes,

2390   And control of the Geats.   There was a king!

He remembered   that fall of his prince

In later days,   became the friend of Eadgils

When his wretchedness came;   supported the son of Ohthere

Among his people   far over the seas

With fighting men, with weapons;   he enjoyed requital,

Cold in his sad journey;   took the king's life.

So he survived   each terrible conflict,

Every battle,   the son of Ecgtheow,

With valor radiant,   until the day came

2400   When it was his   to fight against the serpent.

He went, one of twelve,   enraged in his anger,

This lord of the Geats,   to seek out the dragon;

He had by then heard   how the hostility arose,

The wickedness to his people;   the glorious vessel

Was placed in his lap   by his informant's hand.

He made the thirteenth   of that company of men,

He who had brought about   the beginning of the strife.

Servant sad of mind,   despised he was then,

Had to show them the place.   Against his own will

2410   He took them to the mound   that he alone knew,

A cave under the earth   near the surge of the sea,

Close to the tossing waves;   inside it was full

Of precious treasures and ornaments.   The frightful guardian,

The ready fighter,   held the gold-treasures,

All of them, under the earth;   that was no easy bargain

For any warrior   to secure as his own.

He sat there on the bluff,   that king brave in battle,

And then wished good luck   to his hearth companions,

The gold-giving friend of the Geats.   His spirit was sad

2420　And restless and ready for death.   The fate was close by

That the ancient one   would find as his own,

That would seek out his soul's treasure,   and rend apart

His life from his body.   Not for much longer

Would the noble man's spirit   be at one with his flesh.

　　　　Beowulf spoke,   the son of Ecgtheow:

"Often in my youth   did I endure the storms of battle,

The times of war --   and I remember it all well!

I was seven winters old   when the prince of treasures,

The friend and lord of his people,   took me from my father;

2430　King Hrethel   held me and trained me,

Gave me fortune and feasts,   remembering our kinship,

And never was I to him in life   a whit more estranged

As a child in the castle   than either of his own children,

Herebeald and Haethcyn,   or my own Hygelac!

The eldest of them   was unfittingly slain

By a kinsman's deed,   was sent to his bed of death

When Haethcyn   with a great curved bow,

His friend and lord   struck with an arrow

That missed the mark;   thus did he shoot his closest kin,

2440　His own brother,   with a blood-fated arrow.

No atoning with money   for that exceedingly sore sin,

Blindingly sad it wearies the mind,   -- and still it is,

A prince unavenged   was lost from life.

　　　　So is the sadness   to the aged man,

And grief beyond enduring,   when his young son

Hangs high on the gallows;   then he utters the pain,

Grievous the lamenting,   when his son hangs there

For the joy of the raven,   and aching with age and wisdom,

He might not help him -- can do nothing.

2450 Again and again at morning he is reminded
Of his son's death; he has no desire
To see another alive in the court,
An heir for the treasures, when the first has
So harshly experienced the distress of death.
Sorrowful, he sees in his son's dwelling
The wine-hall deserted, the wind-swept resting-place
So deprived of cheerfulness -- the horseman sleeps,
The warrior in his grave; there is no joy of harp there,
No happiness in the dwelling, as there once was.

2460   He goes then to the bed-stead, singing his song of
sorrow,
One alone after one; and he thinks too spacious by far,
His lands and his castle.

So the defender of the Weders
Enclosed in his heart overwhelming grief
For Herebeald; nor could he at all
Give recompense for the hostility of the life-slayer,
Nor sooner the warrior son could he hate,
Nor do loathsome deeds himself, though he did not love him.
He then with his sorrow in the depths of his spirit
Gave up on the joys of men, chose God's light instead;

2470 And to his sons as does a prosperous man,
He left lands and townships when he departed from life.

Then there was hostility and strife between the Swedes
and the Geats,
Quarrels and mutual hard hostilities
Over the wide waters, when Hrethel lay dead,
And the sons of Ongentheow were
Bold and warlike, and wished no friendship

To hold over the seas,   but around Hreosnabeorh
Dealt out   horrid cruelty and slaughter.
All of that   my kin avenged,
2480 The battles and the hostilities,   as has often been told,
Though the older one   paid with his life,
Hard purchase that was;   Haethcyn was,
Lord of the Geats,   slaughtered in battle.
Then I heard in the morning   my other kin,
With the edge of sword   took revenge on the killer --
When Ongentheow   was attacking Eofor;
In split war-helmet   the ancient Scylfing,
Fallen mortally wounded --   the hand remembered
Enough of the enmity,   and withheld not the deadly blow.
2490   I repaid him   at battle for all
The treasures he gave,   what to me was granted by fate
And gleaming sword;   he gave me land ---
Estate and noble dwelling.   There was no need
That he among the Gifthas   or among the Danes
Or among the Swedes   had to search
For a weaker warrior   to buy with treasure;
Always before him on foot   I wished to go,
Alone on the point,   and so shall I always in life,
In the conflict,   when this sword endures
2500 That earlier and later   often stood by me.
When before my followers   I became the handslayer
Of Daeghrefn,   the champion of the Hugas,
Not at all could he bring back   the treasures,
The breast ornament,   to the Frisian king,
But in battle he fell,   the keeper of the banner,
A nobleman, in valor;   no edge killed him --
But my hostile grip;   it surged his heart,

Broke his rib cage.   Now shall the sword-edge,

The hand and the hard sword,   battle over the treasure."

2510   Beowulf spoke,   uttered a manly boast

For the last time: "I have dared many

Battles in my youth;   yet do I wish,

An old guard of the people,   one last warlike act,

One glorious deed to perform,   if the man-enemy

Will come from the cave   to seek me out."

Then he greeted   each of the men,

Valiant warriors   and dear companions,

This one last time: "I would not carry sword

Nor any weapon to the serpent,   if I knew how

2520   Against the monster   I might else

Grapple in my boast,   as before I did against Grendel.

But there I expect deadly fire,   and heat

In breath and in venom;   and so I take with me

Bright shield, war corselet.   I will not flee a foot of space

From the mound-watcher,   but it shall be for us

There at the wall   as fate grants to us,

The Ruler, as to all.   I am bold in spirit;

Against the battle-flyer.   I boast no further.

Wait you on the barrow,   men in your byrnies,

2530   Warriors in war-gear,   which of us is better able

Between the two of us,   to survive our wounds

After the bloody conflict.   It is not your destiny,

Not proper for any   except for me alone,

To struggle in battle   against the might of the monster,

As proof of manliness.   I with valor shall

Win the treasures,   or in severest fashion

Deadly battle will   seize your lord!"

He arose then with his shield,   the renowned warrior,

Hard in his helmet,   brave in his coat of mail,

2540   Close to the rocky cliffs;   trusted the strength

Of one man alone;   not the way of a coward by far!

Then he who had endured   the thrusts of battle

And the crash of arms,   good in manly virtues

At the clashing of troops,   saw by the wall

A great stone arch standing   and a steam rushing forth,

Bursting out from the barrow;   its waters enraged

With hot deadly fire   -- he could not for even a moment

Approach the hoard   without burning,

Nor get through the hollow   to where the dragon lay.

2550   The lord of the Geats,   when his rage grew,

Let come from his breast   a great wail,

Gave forth a stout-hearted cry;   his voice let sound

A great battle call   there under the gray rock.

Hate was then summoned;   the treasure guardian noted

The man's clear voice;   no time now

For the beseeching of peace.   First there came

The breath of the dragon   out from the rocks,

His hot battle-breath;   the earth trembled!

The hero at the cave,   the lord of the Geats,

2560   Swung his shield   towards the dreadful stranger;

Then the coiled serpent   was impelled by his heart

To seek harsh battle.   The good battle-king

Had before drawn his sword,   the ancient heirloom

With unhesitant edge;   each of the two,

Intending hostility,   was a horror to the other.

When the dragon coiled   quickly together,

The friendly prince   stood stout-hearted and firm

Behind his steep shield;   in his armor he waited.

He came then gliding,   coiled and flaming,

2570   Hastening to his fate.   The shield protected well

The life and body   of the glorious warrior

For less of a time   than he would have hoped;

That day was the first day,   the only time ever

That fate had not   decreed for him

Triumph in battle.   The lord of the Geats

Struck upwards with his hand   with the icy heirloom,

Flailed at the shimmering horror,   but that edge failed him.

Bright sword against bone   could not cut through,

Was less than the king of the people   truly had need of,

2580   Oppressed by this affliction.   After that battle-stroke

The cave-watcher was   savage in his mind,

Belched out murderous fire;   widely sprayed

Battle blazes of flame.   There was to be no victory boast

For the gold-giving Geat.   The war-sword,

Drawn for battle,   failed as it never had done,

Iron for ages excellent.   Nor was that time pleasant

When the strong one,   the kin of Ecgtheow,

The earthly field there   had to give up

Against his will,   had to find dwelling

2590   Elsewhere;   so must each man

Give up at the end of his days.

                         It was not long then

Before the dragon   and the man clashed once more.

The hoard-keeper roused himself;   his breast surged

Again anew.   Surrounded by flames,

He who had led the people   suffered mightily.

Not one of the troop   of his companions,

Of the sons of noblemen   stood by him,

Virtuous in battle,   but they flew to the woods

To save their lives.   Only in one of them welled up

2600	A spirit of sorrow -- the duties of kinship may never
	A whit turn aside in a right thinking man.

Wiglaf he was called,   Weohstan's son,

A beloved shield-warrior,   a Scylfing man,

And kinsman to Aelfhere;   saw that his lord

Behind his war-mask   suffered so from heat.

Then he remembered the riches   he before had given him --

The splendid high hall   of the Waegmundings,

Such folk-shares of land   as his father had held,

And he could not hold back.   His hand seized shield,

2610 Yellow linden-wood.   He drew ancient sword;

It was known to men   as Eanmund's heirloom.

He was Ohthere's son;   adventurer, friendless;

He in battle   was slain by Weohstan,

With battle-edged sword,   who took then to his kinsman

The pale shining helmet,   the ringed war-shirt,

And the ancient giant-wrought sword.   Onela gave back to him

His own kinsman's   war gear,

That ready armor,   and spoke not of the feud,

Although it was his own brother's son   Weohstan had killed.

2620 He then held the treasures   for many winters,

The sword and the byrnie,   until his son could

Act with such nobility   as his father had;

Then, among the Geats,   he gave his son

All of that war dress   when he left this life,

Old, as the old do.   Now was the first time

That the young warrior   would stand to the battle

At the side of his dear lord,   as a warrior should stand.

His mind did not soften,   nor his father's gift

Fail at the battle;   that the dragon found out

2630 When they together   contended in the contest.

Wiglaf spoke,   many right-words

He said to his companions   -- his heart was mournful -- :

"I remember that time   there in the beer hall,

Where we took our mead,   when we vowed

To our lord   who gave us treasures,

That we would repay him   his gifts of war-gear,

Should he have the need,   with helmet

And hard sword.   In choosing he honored us

For this fateful journey,   as he himself willed,

2640 Thought us men fit for glory,   and gave me those rich treasures,

For he considered us spear-carriers   worthy of war,

Vigorous under our helmets --   although the war-lord,

Guardian of the people,   meant to perform

This noble task   alone, unaided,

Because of all men   he had accomplished

The most audacious of deeds.   Now is the day come

When this lord   has need of might

And of good battle warriors;   let us go to him;

Let us help the war-chief,   now that it is

2650 Grim time for fire-terror!   As for me, God knows

I would the sooner   the fire should embrace

My body   with my gold-giving lord.

I think it not proper   that we bear our shields

Again to our homes,   unless first we might

Defend against the foe   and protect the life

Of this Weder leader.   I know readily

That the glory of his former deeds   forbids that he alone

Of the Geatish warriors   should suffer sorrow

And sink at battle;   but sword and helmet,

2660 Byrnie -- all war garments   -- shall be ours together."

He went then through the reeking fumes,   ready under his helmet,

With help for his lord,   and he spoke these few words:
"Beloved Beowulf,   do well all that is to come,
As you so long ago   in your youth said,
That you not endure   during your life
The fall of glory;   you must now with brave deeds,
Strong-hearted nobleman,   and with the whole of your strength,
Defend all.   I am with you."
         After those words   the dragon charged --
2670 Horrible deadly stranger --   yet once more,
Radiant with fire-surge,   attacking his enemies,
Malicious mankind.   Waves of flame
Burned his shield to the boss,   and his byrnie
Could not give help   to the young spear-fighter,
But the courageous man   went bravely in under
His kinsman's shield,   when his own
Was consumed by the flames.   Then again the battle-king,
Mindful of glories,   with great strength struck
With his battle-sword,   and forced by the violence
2680 It struck in the head;   Naegling burst;
Beowulf's sword,   ancient and gray,
Failed at the battle.   It was not to be his
That the two-edged sword   might be of help
To him in that warfare;   it is recounted that his hand
Was too strong   for any of the swords
Which he bore into battle,   hard wondrous weapons.
His strength was overpowering,   and he paid dearly for that.
         Then the spoiler of people,   the audacious fire-dragon,
Was moved to attack   for the third time.
2690 When he saw his chance,   burning and battle-grim,
He once again rushed the brave warrior,   bit into his neck,
Tearing with his tusks;   the warrior was covered with blood.

His life blood   spurted out in great waves.

        Then it is said at the need   of the people's king,

The upright warrior   made known his courage,

His strength and his boldness,   as was his nature.

He made no move for the head,   but this high-spirited man,

His hand badly burned,   struck at the dragon's middle --

Where he stood firm for his leader,   this warrior in war-gear,

2700   So that the sword,   shining and gold plated,

Struck home.   Then after that the fire

Began to subside.   Still the king

Had control of his senses;   he drew his war-knife,

Keen and battle-sharp,   always at his side.

The lord of the Weders   cut deep into the dragon's belly.

The horror was killed   -- their courage had cut it down --

They both together   had finished him off,

These warrior kin.   So should a soldier be --

A thane at the need!   That for the leader was

2710   The last victory battle   of his handiwork

In this world.

        Then the wound

Which the cave-dragon   had inflicted upon him

Began to burn and swell;   he soon knew

That some fatal thing   welled up in his breast,

Some venom within.   Then the noble king,

Wise in his thoughts,   went to the wall

And fell to a seat;   he gazed there at the work of giants,

Saw how the stone arches,   forever supported by columns,

Held the weight   of that ancient earth-cave.

2720   Then the best of the best of thanes   held the glorious

Blood-stained   prince in his arms,

Washed with his own hands   his friendly lord,

So weary of battle,   and unfastened his helmet.

       Beowulf spoke,   said words in spite of his wound,

The wound that would take him;   he knew then

That his day's time was over.   He had passed through

The joys of the earth;   all was finished

Of his day's number,   and death was very near:

"Now to a son   I would have wished to give

2730   This war-dress,   had it been given to me that

An heir   I should have,

Sprung from my body.   I held my people

For fifty winters;   and there was no king of any nation

In all the regions   from any place

Who dared to greet me   with warriors,

Or who threatened us terribly.   I on earth awaited

My destiny,   held my own well,

Sought not any contest,   nor swore any

Unrighteous oaths.   Sick with my mortal wound,

2740   All of this I may   now hold in joy;

For the Ruler of men   will have no need

To blame me for the murder of kin,   when life has departed

From my body.   Now go you quickly

To examine the hoard   under the gray rock,

Beloved Wiglaf,   now that the serpent lies

With his death wounds,   deprived of his treasures.

Be now in haste,   that I the ancient wealth,

The golden things may see,   may eagerly examine,

Brilliant precious jewels,   so that the more softly

2750   After the wealth of treasures   I may give up

My life and my country,   which I have held so long."

       Then as it is related,   the son of Weohstan,

After hearing the words   of the wounded

Battle-weary lord,   hurried in his coat of mail,

The woven ringed-net,   down under the mound.

The victorious one saw,   after he had passed the seat,

Courageous young retainer,   precious pale jewels,

Glittering gold,   lying there,

Wonders on the wall,   and the dragon's den,

2760   Ancient dawn-flyer,   and cups standing,

Vessels of men of old,   long without polisher,

Deprived of their jewels.   There were many helmets,

Ancient and rusty,   and scores of arm-bracelets,

Twisted with skill.   Too easily can riches,

Gold in the ground,   overpower

Any one of mankind,   hide it who will!

He also saw there   a banner all of gold,

High over the hoard,   hand-wrought in high wonders,

Interwoven skillfully;   from it a light gleamed out,

2770   So that he could see   the floor of the barrow,

See clearly the works of art.   There was no sign

Of the dragon now;   the sword had taken it.

Then it is said that,   alone in the barrow

He plundered the hoard,   the antique work of giants;

Gathered to his bosom   the drinking vessels and plates

That he thought the best;   he also took the standard,

The brightest of banners.   Beowulf's good sword,

-- the edge was iron --   had before harmed

The guardian of the hoard,   he who held the treasures

2780   For time beyond telling,   kept the fire-terror

Flaming, raging fiercely   at the hoard entrance

In the dark of the night   until he was slain and died.

The good retainer was in haste,   eager to return;

He advanced with the precious things.   Curiosity tormented him,

Whether he would find   the bold of spirit,

The lord of the Geats,   deprived of strength,

Still alive in that place   where he left him.

Carrying the treasures   he found his lord,

The glorious prince,   bloody, and at the end

2790   Of his life.   He tried once again

To clean him with water,   until pointed words

Broke through to his heart.

The hero-king spoke,

Ancient in sorrow,   as he beheld the gold:

"For all these precious things   that I here gaze upon,

I thank the Lord of all,   the King of the world,

The eternal Ruler,   while I yet have words --

That I might   have secured such things

For my people   before the day of my death.

Now that I have bought   the treasures of this hoard

2800   With my old life,   attend now to the needs

Of the people;   I will not be with you for long.

Order the great battle-warriors   to build a splendid barrow,

After the funeral pyre,   at the point by the sea,

As a reminder   to my people.

It shall tower high   as Hronesness,

So that seafarers forever after   shall call it

Beowulf's barrow,   when the ships

Over the dark waters   come from afar."

Then he took the golden collar   from his neck,

The bold-minded prince,   and gave it to the warrior,

To the young spear-fighter,   and the gold-adorned helmet,

His rings and his byrnie,   and implored him to use them well -- :

"You are the last remnant   of our family,

A Waegmunding: fate has swept away all

Of my kinsmen   to what it decreed for them,
Noblest of warriors;   I shall soon follow."
That was the last word   of the old man,
From his depths of his heart,   before he tasted the pyre,
Hot hostile flames;   his soul quickly departed
2820   From his body   to seek righteous judgment.
            Then it happened   to the young man
Sorrowfully,   that he on the earth saw
The most loved man,   his life at an end,
Pitiably lying there.   His slayer also lay close,
Terrible earth-dragon,   deprived of his life,
Utterly destroyed.   Never again
Would the coiled serpent   guard the ring-hoard,
But the two-edged sword   had taken him,
Hard, battle-sharp,   hammered heirloom;
2830   So that the wide-flyer,   stilled with wounds,
Fell to earth   near the treasure house.
Nor ever again would he   fly through the air
In the black of night,   glorying in his treasures,
Proud of his appearance,   but he fell to earth
Because of the handiwork   of the war chief.
No man it seems   who in this land
Is sufficiently mighty,   if the truth be told,
No matter his daring,   the valor of his deeds,
Could survive the venomous breath   of the hideous foe,
2840   Could in the ring-hall   with his hands overcome,
If he discovered,   found awake and ready,
The guard of the cave.   Beowulf became
The lord of those treasures   with payment of his life;
Each of the foes   had reached the end
Of this transitory life.

It was not long then
Before the cowards   skulked out of the woods,
The weak traitors,   ten together,
Who before had not dared   to fly their spears
In their war-lord's   greatest of needs;
2850   Consumed by shame   they bore their shields,
And their linked armor   to where the ancient one lay.
They stared silently at Wiglaf.   He sat weary of spirit,
Splendid foot-soldier,   near the king's shoulder;
He tried water again to waken him,   but knew it would fail.
No way in all the world,   although he ached to succeed,
To keep alive   his glorious chieftain,
Nor to change the will   of the Ruler of all;
God's judgment   controlled the deeds
Of each man then,   and He now still does.
2860   Then came grim words   by the young retainer,
Easy to say   to those who before had lost courage.
Wiglaf spoke,   Weohstan's son,
To the wretched men   -- eyeing the unfaithful -- :
"Who speaks the truth   might easily say
That the liege-lord   who gave you treasures,
Such war equipment   that you stand in even now,
When he at the ale-bench   often dispensed such things
To the hall-sitters,   helmets and byrnies,
Great prince to his thanes,   most splendid gifts that he
2870   Either far or near   had found -- ,
That such war dress   he had completely, grievously
Thrown away,   when war had come to him,
No cause at all   could the people-king find
To boast of his war comrades!   However, the eternal God,
The Ruler of Victory,   wished that he himself know victory,

Alone with his sword,   when he had need of courage.

To save his life   I could do little,

Give little at battle,   yet still I tried,

Whatever my skills,   to help my kinsman.

2880   The deadly foe   moved always the slower

With each strike of my sword,   the fire less violent

That surged from his head.   Too few strong arms

Thronged about the prince   when that hardship fell to him.

Now shall the receiving of treasure,   the giving of swords,

High joy in estate,   and comfort cease

For all of your kinsmen;   land rights shall lapse

For every one   of your people

When warriors and noblemen   listen afar

To the story   of your flight,

2890   Your inglorious deeds.   Death is better

For any man   than a life of disgrace!"

He ordered then that   the battle-work be proclaimed

Up over the edge of the cliff   where the band of warriors,

Sat, sad of heart,   for the length of the morning,

Their shields close,   ready at once,

Expecting the end   of their hero's days

Or his return.   He who rode up the hill

With the news   was hardly silent;

He told the whole of the tale,   spoke the truth to all within hearing:

2900   "Now is the giver of joy   to the Weder people,

The lord of the Geats,   fast in his bed of death;

He lies slaughtered,   the deed of the dragon.

Lying at his side   is the old adversary,

Dead of dagger wounds;   with his sword he could not

Mark the monster,   cause a wound

Of any sort.   Wiglaf sits

Close by the side of Beowulf;   he is Weohstan's son,

Consumed with sorrow,   living warrior

Keeping watch over dead warrior;   he holds guard

2910   Over the beloved and the hostile.

                                    Now can the people expect

A time for war --   after it becomes

Widely known   to the Franks and the Frisians

That the king has fallen.   That strife was begun

Hard against the Hugas   when Hygelac came,

Bringing his naval force   to the Frisian land;

There the Hetware   moved against him in harsh battle,

Vigorously fought   with greater numbers,

So that the mailed-warrior   suffered defeat,

Fell in the midst of his own troops;   no treasure there

2920   For his own trusted retainers.   To us after that

The Frankish king   extended no kindness.

                        Nor have I hope   for peace or trust

Among the Swedish people,   for it was not difficult to know

That Ongentheow   deprived Haethcyn of his life,

Hrethel's son,   near Ravenswood,

When in their arrogance   the Geatish people

First sought   the battle Scylfings.

At once Ohthere's father,   ancient and violent,

Gave requital to them   for that deed

2930   When he destroyed the sea-king,   set free his wife,

Ancient woman   deprived of gold,

Onela's mother,   and Ohthere's;

He followed them then,   his deadly foes,

Until they escaped   into Ravenswood,

Full of anguish   in lacking a lord.

He surrounded them with a huge force,   the battle leavings,

Weary of their wounds,   and frightened
The wretched company   all the night long;
Said he would kill some in the morning   with sword's edge,
2940   Hang some from   the gallows tree
For the sport of the birds.   Consolation suddenly came
To their weary spirits   with the light of day,
When they caught   the clear sound
Of Hygelac's horn and trumpet,   when the good prince
Came down the path   with his best retainers.

That bloody track   of Swedes and Geats
Trailing slaughtered men   was widely seen --
How the two warrior tribes   stirred up the hostilities.
Then the ancient one,   this man Ongentheow,
2950   Solemn and wise,   with his kinsmen
Moved further up   in seeking a stronghold;
He had heard   of Hygelac's battle-prowess,
His high-spirited war-skills,   and did not trust resistance,
Did not feel   that he could withstand
This renowned sea-warrior,   or defend his treasure,
His sons or his wife.   Then he turned,
Old, to his earthen fortress.   Then chase was offered
To the Swedish men --   Hygelac's banners
Flew forthrightly   over the field,
2960   Once Hrethel's men   attacked the enclosure.
There Ongentheow,   old and gray,
By the force of sword   was brought to task,
So that the Swedish people-king   had to submit
To Eofor's single judgment.   Angrily Wulf,
The son of Wonred,   lashed out with his sword,
Struck well enough   that blood spurted forth
From the old man's forehead.   It did not stop

The revered Scylfing;   he quickly requited

With a harsher blow,   dealt the slash of slaughter

2970   When the people-king   whirled towards him.

The brave son of Wonred   had no answer

For that stroke   of the old warrior;

He had cut clear through   the other's helmet,

So that drenched in blood   he had to fall

To the harsh earth   -- not yet doomed,

For he would recover --   but beyond fighting.

Then the brave one,   Hygelac's thane,

When his brother lay there writhing,   took his broad sword,

Let crash the giant-made weapon   into the great helmet,

2980   Broke in over the protecting shield;   the king dropped,

The people's protector,   struck from this life.

Then there were many   who would bind up his kinsman

And raise him to standing,   once there was room

And they had control   of the battle-field.

Then one warrior   plundered the other,

Took the iron-mail coat   from Ongentheow's dead body,

His great hilted sword,   and his helmet as well,

All ancient armor,   and brought them to Hygelac.

He received the precious armor   and fittingly called

2990   For reward for him once they were home,   and fulfilled it so;

The lord of the Geats,   Hrethel's son,

When he returned to his house   gave the battle-attackers,

Eofor and Wulf,   plenty of treasures,

Gave to them property,   a hundred thousand

In lands and locked-ring things;   no need to blame him for that payment

By any man on earth,   because they had slain the glorious one;

And then he gave to Eofor   his own daughter

As ornament for his home,   to wed in friendship.

That is the feud   and the enmity,
3000   The hostility of men,   for which I expect
The Swedish people   will seek us out
When they learn   that our king
Is lifeless;   he who before held the ground
Against the enemy,   kept hoard and riches
Following the death   of the valiant Scyldings,
Worked for the benefit   of the people.
And did so nobly.   Now is haste best
So that we may there behold   the king of the people,
And then bring him   who gave us rings
3010   To the funeral pyre.   Not one thing alone shall melt
With the brave one,   but the whole treasure hoard itself,
Countless gold   so grimly purchased;
And now at the last   the treasures bought
With his own life,   now shall the burning consume them,
The fire enfold them,   not a warrior will wear them
As precious remembrances,   nor fair woman
Shall have the ringed ornaments   about her neck;
But sad of mind,   deprived of gold,
They shall tread the far country   more often than once,
3020   Now that the war-leader   has laid down laughter,
And joy, and mirth.   The war-spear shall be
Grasped by many   morning-cold hands,
Hands by the score;   and no joy of harp
To still the warrior,   but the dark raven,
Ready over the dead,   will speak much,
Will say to the eagle   how he came to the banquet,
When he and the wolf   plundered the battlefield."
Thus did the valiant man   speak aloud
His loathsome story;   he voiced only the truth

3030   Of events and words.   The whole band rose
        And went sorrowfully   under Earnaness,
        Awash with tears,   to examine that wonder.
        They found then on the sand,   lying there lifeless,
        Held in his bed of rest,   he who gave them rings
        In earlier times.   There was come the end of days
        For that good warrior,   -- when the battle king,
        The prince of the Weders,   was killed in a dreadful death.
        Just before a stranger   they had seen there,
        A dragon at the place   lying there opposite.
3040   Enveloped in hostility;   the fire dragon
        Was grimly terrible,   its color burned in flames;
        It was fifty   feet in length
        As it lay there.   For a time air-joyous,
        It held the nights,   then downward it went
        To visit its den;   and now death took hold.
        It had enjoyed   the last of its earth cavern.
        By it stood   cups and flagons,
        And dishes lay there,   and precious swords
        Eaten through with rust,   because they lay in earth's embrace,
3050   And had remained so   for a thousand winters.
        Then was that heritage   exceedingly huge,
        Gold of ancient men   wound in a spell,
        So that the ring-vault   no man could
        Break into,   unless God himself,
        The true King of Victory,   gave to one He wished
          -- He is the protector of men --   to open the treasure hoard,
        And only to such a man   as He thought proper.
              Then it was seen   that it could not pay
        For the unholy one   who within secretly kept
3060   Art treasures under the wall;   the guardian first slew

One of a few only;   and that hostile act was

Then severely avenged.   A wonder the time

When the brave warrior   goes at the end

Of his fated life,   when he no longer may

Dwell with his kinsmen,   glad in the mead-hall!

And so it was with Beowulf   when he sought the barrow-guard

And a treacherous quarrel;   he did not know

What his parting from this world   was destined to be,

So until doom's day   was the solemn curse

3070   By the glorious princes   who placed the treasure;

The man who   plundered that place

Would be guilty of sin,   with evil tormented,

Should be fast in the bonds of hell,   and restrained by idols.

By no means greedy for gold,   but more eagerly

The Lord's good will,   he sought to have.

Wiglaf spoke,   Weohstan's son:

"Often shall many men   endure misery

For the will of one,   as is now ours to do.

We could not persuade   our beloved prince,

3080   Keeper of the kingdom,   with any council,

That he should not   meet the gold-guardian,

But should let him lie   where he had lain for so long,

To remain in that barrow   to the end of the world.

He held to high-destiny;   the hoard is laid open,

But grim the victory.   That lure of fate was too strong

Which impelled the king of our people   to that place.

I went in myself,   looked over it all,

All the treasure in that hall,   when I had my chance;

Not easy my fate   when I was allowed to visit

3090   In under the earth dome.   In haste I seized,

Grasped in my hands   a mighty burden

Of riches from the hoard;   I bore it all out here

To my king.   He was still alive,

Conscious and wise,   and spoke of much,

Old in his sorrow;   and then he ordered me to greet you,

Bade that you make   tribute to a friend's deeds,

At the place of the pyre,   the highest of mounds,

Great in its glory,   because he was a man,

The most worthy of warriors   over all of the earth,

3100   When he could enjoy   the wealth of a castle.

Let us now hasten   yet once more

To seek out and to examine   the heap of precious jewels,

Wondrous under the wall.   I will show you the way

So that near, you can see   sufficient of the riches

And the broad gold.   Make the bier ready,

Prepare it speedily   when we come out,

And then let us go   with our king,

Beloved man,   to where he long shall

Abide in the Ruler's protection."

3110   Then Weohstan's son,   the battle-famed hero,

Issued the order   to many warriors,

Owners of dwellings,   that such carry from afar

Wood for the funeral pyre,   these chiefs of the people,

To where the good man lay: "Now the flames shall consume,

The dark fire shall thrive   on this chief warrior,

He who often survived   iron-showers,

When storms of arrows,   sent with might,

Passed over shield-walls,   thrust on by the shafts,

Trued by their feathers --   serving the arrowheads."

3120   And now the wise   son of Weohstan

Summoned from   the king's thanes,

Seven all told,   the best of the best.

And the eight of them,   soldiers all,

Moved in under the evil roof;   the one who went in front

Bore a torch   in his hand.

There was no concern for shares   by the men who then plundered

the hoard,

After they saw   the precious pieces

Untended by the guardian   strewn about the hall,

Lying there transitory.   And little any mourned

3130   That they speedily   hurried away then

With those precious treasures.   First they pushed the dragon,

The serpent, over the cliff wall,   and let the waves take him.

They let the flood embrace   the herder of treasures.

Then all the twisted gold   was laid in a wagon,

Countless of all things.   The hero was borne,

The old battle-warrior,   to Hronesness.

The Geatish people   then made ready for him

A funeral pyre on the earth;   it was a splendid thing --

With war-helmets, and battle-shields,

3140   And bright byrnies,   all as he had wished.

And then the warriors,   lamenting their beloved lord,

Lay the illustrious prince   there at the center.

The men then began   the largest of funeral pyres

On those cliffs;   the wood smoke curled

Black over the flames;   the roaring of the fire

Mingled with the weeping   -- the wind tumult subsided --

Until the heat had   broken the body,

Melted the breast.   In depressed spirits

They uttered soul-sorrow   at the death of their lord.

3150   And as well a mournful song   keened in deep sorrow

Came from an old woman   with bound-up hair;

Sung in anguish,   told earnestly

That she dreaded   her hard evil days to come,

Filled with great slaughter   and terror of warriors,

Indignities and captivity.   Smoke swallowed the sky.

The men of the Weders   then made,

There on the hill,   high and broad

And widely visible   to traveling seafarers,

Built in the space   of ten days,

3160   The memorial to the battle-bold one,   and surrounded with a wall

The leavings of the flames,   the most splendid that

The wisest of men   were able to devise.

On the mound they put   the rings and jewels,

And all such ornaments   that hostile enemies

Had taken from there,   had stolen from the hoard.

The men abandoned the treasure   for the earth to hold,

The gold to the earth,   where it now yet lies,

As useless to men   as it ever was.

Then about the mound   rode the battle-brave ones,

3170   The sons of princes,   twelve in all,

Who wished to speak of care,   and to lament for their king,

To recite elegies   and to speak about his story.

They praised his manhood   and his noble works,

And lauded his excellence   -- for it is fitting

That a man honor his lord and friend   with words,

And love him from his heart,   when his spirit

Shall be led forth   from his body.

So the Geatish people,   his hearth companions,

Deeply lamented   their fallen lord;

3180   They said that he was   of all world kings,

The mildest of men,   and the gentlest,

The kindest to his people,   and the most eager for praise.

SOME PROMINENT NAMES in *BEOWULF*

* *

The number following each name represents the line of the poem where the name first appears.

Aelfhere   (2604) – Kinsman of Wiglaf.

Aeschere   (1323) – One of Hrothgar's counselors, murdered and carried off by Grendel's mother.

Beowulf   (343) – Hero of the poem. He is a warrior of the highest heroic standards. He slays Grendel, Grendel's mother, and with the help of Wiglaf, a great dragon. Rules for fifty years.

Breca   (506) – Loses an impetuous but nonetheless heroic swimming contest against Beowulf.

Brondings   (521) – Breca's people.

Brosings   (1199) – One of the tribes mentioned in the poem, owners of the great necklace said to be stolen by Hama.

Daeghrefn   (2502) – Frisian warrior slain in battle by Beowulf.

Earnaness   (3031) – high promontory near to the site of the battle between Beowulf (and Wiglaf) and the dragon.

Ecglaf   (499) – The Dane, father of Unferth.

Ecgtheow   (263) – Father of Beowulf.

Ecgwela   (1710) – One of the Danish kings.

Eofor   (2486) – Great warrior, the slayer of the old king Ongentheow.

Eomer   (1960) – Son of Offa.

Eormenric   (1201) – King of the East Goths, committed suicide.

Finn   (1068) – King of the Finns.

Fitela   (879) – Nephew and fighting companion of Sigemund.

Folcwalda   (1090) – Father of Finn.

Freawaru   (2023) – Daughter to Hrothgar, given in marriage to Ingeld.

Froda   (2025) – Chief of the Heathobards and father of Ingeld.

Garmund   (1962) – Father of Offa.

Geats   (195) – Tribe of Swedish people, ultimately ruled by Beowulf; secondarily known in the poem as Weders.

Grendel   (102) – Manlike monster, descended from Cain. He is a ravaging murderer who attacks Heorot and violently kills its warriors. He is killed by Beowulf.

Haereth   (1929) – Father of Hygd.

Haethcyn   (2434) – Second son of Hrethel; killed by Ongentheow at Ravenswood.

Halga   (61) – Younger brother of Hrothgar.

Hama   (1198) – From the Gothic cycle of legends; steals the famous Brosing necklace.

Healfdene   (57) – King of the Danes; son of Danish king Beowulf; father of Hrothgar.

Heardred   (2202) – Geatish king; succeeded to the throne by Beowulf.

Heathobards   (2032) – Germanic tribe to which Ingeld belongs.

Heatholaf   (460) – Wylfing warrior, killed by Beowulf's father, starting a great feud, which Hrothgar settles.

Helmings   (620) – Family to which Wealhtheow (wife of Hrothgar) belongs.

Heorogar   (61) – Danish king, brother of Hrothgar.

Heorot   (78) – Royal Danish hall of Hrothgar; scene of Beowulf's conflict with Grendel.

Heoroweard   (2161) – Son of Heorogar.

Herebeald   (2434) – Eldest son of Hrethel; killed by his brother.

Heremod   (901) – Early Danish king of little worth; he is contrasted with Beowulf.

Hildeburh   (1071) – Daughter of Hoc and wife of the Frisian King Finn.

Hondscio   (2076) – The only Geat killed by Grendel, devoured by him before the battle with Beowulf in Heorot.

Hreosnabeorh   (2477) – A hill in Geat country.

Hrethel   (374) – Geatish king, father of Hygelac, grandfather of Beowulf.

Hrethric   (1189) – Oldest son of Hrothgar.

Hronesness   (2805) – Great promontory where Beowulf wishes his burial-mound to be.

Hrothgar   (61) – Danish king, builder of Heorot; he is anguished by the constant attacks of Grendel, is saved by Beowulf.

Hrothmund   (1189) – Younger son of Hrothgar.

Hrothulf   (1014) –The younger brother of Hrothgar.

Hrunting   (1456) – Unferth's sword; he lends it to Beowulf to aid in the fight against Grendel's mother; it is useless.

Hygd   (1926) – Young wife of Hygelac.

Hygelac   (194) – King of the Geats, uncle to Beowulf.

Ingeld   (2064) – Prince of the Heathobards, son of Froda.

Naegling   (2680) – Beowulf's sword.

Offa   (1951) – King of the continental Angles. Thrith's husband.

Ohthere   (2380) – Son of Swedish king Ongentheow.

Onela   (62) – Son of Swedish king Ongentheow.

Ongentheow   (1968) – Swedish king, father of Ohthere and Onela; killed by Eofor near Ravenswood.

Oslaf   (1148) – Danish warrior who fought against Finn.

Scefing   (4) – Appellation of Scyld.

Scyld   (4) – Mythical Danish king.

Scylfings   (2381) – Swedish dynasty.

Sigemund   (875) – Son of Waels, uncle of Fitela; one the greatest warriors in literature.

Thryth   (1931) – wife of the Anglo king Offa.

Unferth   (499) – Courtier at the court of Hrothgar.

Waegmunding   (2607) – Family to which Weohstan, Wiglaf, and Beowulf belong.

Waels   (897) – Father of Sigemund.

Wayland   (455) – Famous smith of Germanic legend.

Wealhtheow   (612) – Hrothgar's queen.

Weohstan   (2602) – Father of Wiglaf.

Wiglaf   (2602) – A Waegmunding, kinsman of Beowulf.

Withergyld   (2052) – A Heathobard warrior.

Wulf   (2964) – A Geat warrior.

Wulfgar   (348) – An official at the court of Hrothgar.

Yrmenlaf   (1324) A Dane, younger brother of Aeschere.

END

David Kaufman, a retired university professor, holds advanced degrees from both the University of Pittsburgh and Carnegie Mellon University. He has published both short fiction (much of it subsequently anthologized), and non-fiction, and was awarded a life membership as a Technical Associate in THE SOCIETY OF WIRELESS PIONEERS for his series of articles about a linguistic approach to the learning of Morse Code.

www.ingramcontent.com/pod-product-compliance
Lightning Source LLC
Chambersburg PA
CBHW052145170626
46812CB00004B/1593